"Holy Maloney,

"And here I am, think

months is such a pleasure," Mac responded.

"Yes, well, you haven't seen that much of me yet," Abbie said.

"How have you been since...December?"

Abbie's blue eyes shifted doubtfully to him, she opened her mouth, closed it again, then sucked in a deep breath, squared her shoulders and said in a rush, "Pregnant. How have you been?"

Mac's smile faded, along with the excitement and possibility that seeing her again had evoked. *Pregnant?* Had she said...? "Pregnant?" he said, his gut clenching in protest as his gaze dropped helplessly to her midsection.

"Pregnant," she confirmed, thrusting the suitcase at him and revealing the unmistakably rounded contours of her belly beneath the oversize white shirt. "Congratulations, it's yours."

Dear Reader,

This month, Harlequin American Romance delivers your favorite authors and irresistible stories of heart, home and happiness that will surely leave you smiling.

TEXAS SHEIKHS, Harlequin American Romance's scintillating continuity series about a Texas family with royal Arabian blood, continues with *His Shotgun Proposal* by Karen Toller Whittenburg. When Abbie Jones surprised Mac Coleman with the news of her pregnancy, honor demanded he give her his name. But could he give his shotgun bride his heart?

Another wonderful TOTS FOR TEXANS romance from bestselling author Judy Christenberry is in store for you this month with *Struck by the Texas Matchmakers*, in which two children in need of a home and several meddling ladies play matchmakers for a handsome doctor and a beautiful lawyer. Harlequin American Romance's theme promotion, THE WAY WE MET...AND MARRIED, about marriage-of-convenience romances, begins this month with *Bachelor-Auction Bridegroom* by Mollie Molay. And old passions heat up in Leandra Logan's *Family: The Secret Ingredient* when Grace North's first crush, now a single father, returns to town with his precocious little girl and ends up staying under the heroine's roof.

Enjoy this month's offerings and come back next month for more stories guaranteed to touch your heart!

Wishing you happy reading,

Melissa Jeglinski
Associate Senior Editor
Harlequin American Romance

TEXAS SHEIKHS:
HIS SHOTGUN PROPOSAL

Karen Toller Whittenburg

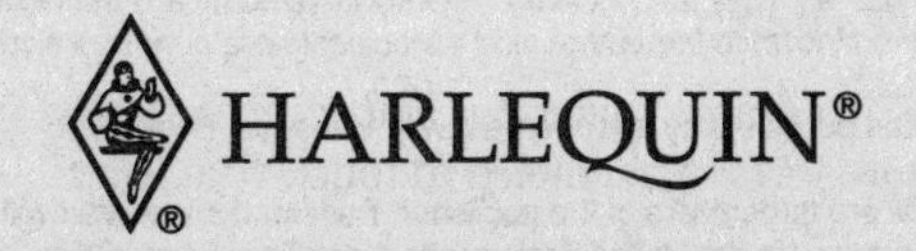

TORONTO • NEW YORK • LONDON
AMSTERDAM • PARIS • SYDNEY • HAMBURG
STOCKHOLM • ATHENS • TOKYO • MILAN • MADRID
PRAGUE • WARSAW • BUDAPEST • AUCKLAND

Special thanks and acknowledgment are given to Karen Toller Whittenburg for her contribution to the TEXAS SHEIKHS series.

Special thank-you to Arron Spradling of Flying "G" Equestrian Services, Lotsee, Oklahoma, for her expert advice on training Arabian horses.

ISBN 0-373-16877-2

HIS SHOTGUN PROPOSAL

This edition published by arrangement with Harlequin Books S.A.

Visit us at www.eHarlequin.com

Printed in U.S.A.

ABOUT THE AUTHOR

Karen Toller Whittenburg is a native Oklahoman who fell in love with books the moment she learned to read and has been addicted to the written word ever since. She wrote stories as a child, but it wasn't until she discovered romance fiction that she felt compelled to write, fascinated by the chance to explore the positive power of love in people's lives. She grew up in Sand Springs (a historic town on the Arkansas River), attended Oklahoma State University and now lives in Tulsa with her husband, a professional photographer.

Books by Karen Toller Whittenburg

HARLEQUIN AMERICAN ROMANCE

197—SUMMER CHARADE
249—MATCHED SET
294—PEPPERMINT KISSES
356—HAPPY MEDIUM
375—DAY DREAMER
400—A PERFECT PAIR
424—FOR THE FUN OF IT
475—BACHELOR FATHER
528—WEDDING OF HER DREAMS
552—THE PAUPER AND THE PRINCESS
572—NANNY ANGEL
621—MILLION-DOLLAR BRIDE*
630—THE FIFTY-CENT GROOM*
648—TWO-PENNY WEDDING*
698—PLEASE SAY "I DO"
708—THE SANTA SUIT
727—A BACHELOR FALLS
745—IF WISHES WERE...WEDDINGS
772—HOW TO CATCH A COWBOY
794—BABY BY MIDNIGHT?
822—LAST-MINUTE MARRIAGE
877—HIS SHOTGUN PROPOSAL

*The Magic Wedding Dress

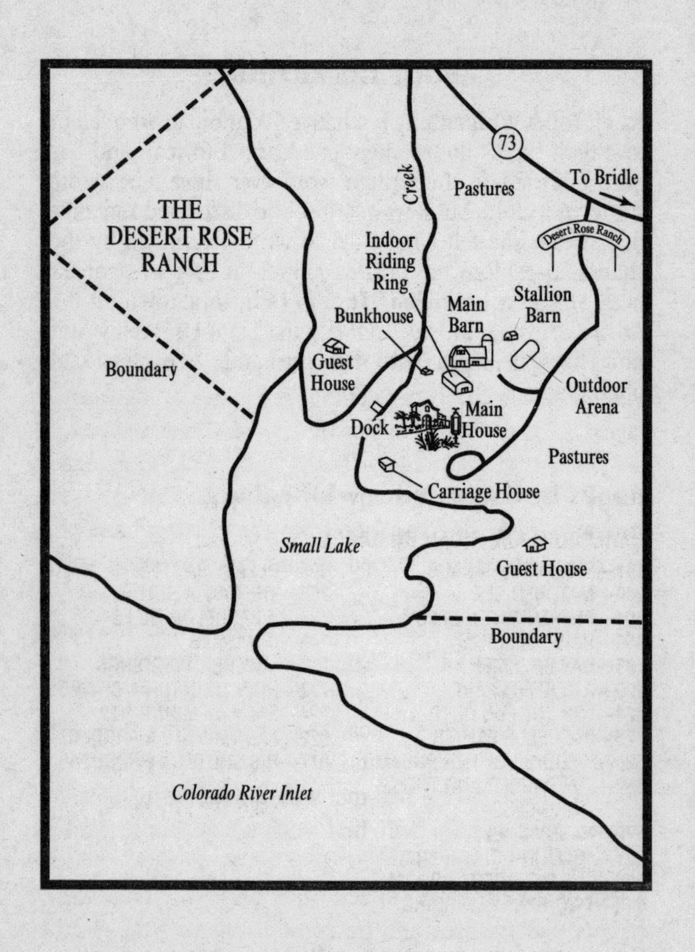

THE DESERT ROSE RANCH
73
To Bridle
Creek
Pastures
Desert Rose Ranch
Indoor Riding Ring
Main Barn
Stallion Barn
Bunkhouse
Guest House
Boundary
Outdoor Arena
Dock
Main House
Pastures
Carriage House
Small Lake
Guest House
Boundary
Colorado River Inlet

Chapter One

A steady stream of travelers lugged baggage of every shape, size and color out of the air-cooled Austin airport and into the muggy Texas heat. Mac Coleman tugged the brim of his cowboy hat down low on his forehead, shielding his face from the blazing haze of afternoon sun as he leaned against his Silverado and watched for his passenger. Not that he had even a faint hope of recognizing her. He'd been *volunteered* to pick up Abigail Jones because he had business in the city on the day she was scheduled to arrive and because his cousin, Jessica, had an annoying way of getting around arguments. His last-ditch effort to avoid chauffeur duty had met with a confident "Don't worry, Mac, Abbie will find you. I told her to look for a scowling cowboy next to a black truck."

His wasn't the only black truck parked outside the baggage claim area and he certainly wasn't the only man wearing a Stetson, but if she showed, he was here. And if not? Well, he'd wait a reasonable while, then head back to the ranch. Visitors to the Desert Rose weren't his responsibility and he planned to keep it that way.

A sassy blonde passed him, displaying enough leg and flirty tosses of her tresses to attract his attention. He watched her sashay by, caught the full effect of the smile she flashed not quite accidentally in his direction and touched the brim of his hat in the half hope she might be his pickup.

She changed direction and came back toward him, tugging her sunglasses down the bridge of her nose and giving him a thorough looking over from above the tortoiseshell frames. He could all but hear her internal calculator *chi-ching* as her glance moved past him to note the Desert Rose crest on the side of the truck and then quickly returned to take in what his older brother, Alex, laughingly called the Coleman ask-me-the-size-of-my-ranch look. ''Do you know where I might find the Four Seasons shuttle?'' she asked in a sultry voice, lightly stressing the name of the hotel.

Okay, so she wasn't Abigail Jones, who wouldn't be asking for a ride to an Austin hotel. But that was just as well. He had enough four-legged fillies to take up his time and attention this summer, as it was, and he didn't need any other distractions. Especially not of this variety. ''No, ma'am,'' he said without regret. ''Can't say that I do.''

''I suppose I could take a cab to the hotel,'' she said with another toothy blaze of a smile. ''Unless I get a...better offer.'' She tossed her hair again...a fine, sun-streaked mane of it, too. Her legs were long and lean, her body slender and supple. No two ways about it, she was candy for the eyes, and had exactly the sort of California looks he most admired. He wished he was interested—he really did—but in truth, he wasn't even tempted to raise the brim of his hat for a better view.

"I sure hope you get that offer, ma'am," he drawled, not giving an inch of encouragement...or discouragement, either, for that matter. "'Cause it's a fair piece of walking to get from here to downtown Austin."

She pouted, as he'd expected she would, unconvinced as yet that with a bit more encouragement he wouldn't be hers for the asking. Women, he'd discovered over the course of his thirty years, could be as predictable as a hill country armadillo and just about as faithless. "Married?" she asked point-blank.

That made him smile. "No, and never going to be."

That made her smile. "Really? Well, it just so happens, I prefer men who have strong opinions about matrimony...one way or the other."

Another time, another place, he might have taken her up on her thinly disguised offer, escorted this sun-bleached beauty to her hotel and stayed over for breakfast. But for the past several months, he'd been hung up on a mysterious lady who had seduced and deserted him all within the span of one incredible night. A short, sandy-haired, blue-eyed elf of a woman who continued to intrude on opportunities such as this with annoying regularity. A slip of a gal, whose name he hadn't been able to discover, whose vanishing act was still as inexplicable to him as her appearance in his hotel room that night last winter, and whose throaty laughter had echoed in all his dreams since. He was damned tired of thinking about her, too, but somehow this just didn't seem the right moment to prove it.

The blonde took off her sunglasses and sucked lightly on one plastic-and-wire earpiece. ''Is *everything* in Texas this *hot?*'' she asked, eyeing him suggestively.

Mac offered her a lazy smile, appreciating her efforts, futile as he'd decided they ultimately would be. ''Oh, no, ma'am. Some things in Texas are a whole lot hotter.''

ABBIE WRESTLED her red plaid suitcase off the steel-jawed baggage carousel and let it fall with a thud on top of the two other bags she'd already rescued—one medium-sized black faux leather and one large faded sea-green paisley. Turning back, she scanned the conveyance for the remaining suitcase, a brown tweed with gray stripes. Well, in truth, the stripes were duct tape, fashioned by Tyler, the youngest of her four older brothers, as a gag gift for her graduation from grad school last December. She had a matched set of brothers and luggage at home, a four-piece, stair-step assortment of each. But for this trip, she'd had to make do with suitcases borrowed helter-skelter, because she didn't want anyone in her family to know this time away from them was going to last considerably longer than she'd led them all to believe. The truth of the matter was she'd told some major whoppers just to get here without them finding out where she was going or why.

It was embarrassing to think she'd gone from

magna cum laude in December to magna cum baby in May, losing the perfect job along the way. She'd had the world on a string, a prestigious teaching position, a future bright with promise, and independence within her grasp. But her fall from grace had been swift and humiliating, even if only a few people knew about it at this point. Everyone would know soon enough. She supposed she should have gone straight home after she'd been fired from Miss Amelia's Academy for Young Ladies, but she just couldn't bring herself to face her parents with the truth. Not yet, anyway.

And if her brothers knew…well, that didn't bear thinking about. If they had even a faint suspicion of the mess she was in, the four of them would descend like warrior angels to fight for her honor and protect her from all harm, even if they suffocated her in the process. They meant well, Tyler, Jaz, Brad and Quinn, in their big-brotherly ways, but if it were up to them, she'd never make a single decision for herself. They'd do it all, they'd do it their way, and they'd do it for her own good. Oh, she loved her rowdy brothers with all her heart, and she hadn't liked having to scheme and plan and plot her way into having a life of her own, but it had been the only way to escape their overly protective and bullheaded-times-four, brothers-know-best attitude.

Of course, practically the very second she'd managed to claim her independence and get out on her own, she'd gotten herself into quite a pickle. But the longer she could keep the family ignorant of her dilemma, the more choices she could keep open for evaluation. There were some decisions a woman had to make for herself, and it was not selfish to want a little bit of peace and quiet while she made them, either.

So if that meant traveling with borrowed and battered suitcases, and throwing herself on the kind and generous aegis of her college friend, Jessica Coleman, so be it. Sooner or later, a person had to cut those apron strings and Abbie's time to *snip, snip, snip* had come. Her plans were a little loose at the moment, but a week or two at the Desert Rose would give her time to figure out what to do next and how, exactly, she was going to tell her father, mother and four burly brothers about this unexpected and completely embarrassing dilemma.

They wouldn't kill the guy who'd gotten her pregnant, because she would never tell them who he was. Not because he deserved her protection, but because she didn't know who he was, either. Just the thought of that night, of hot kisses and wild passion made her skin tingle with a thousand memories, made her shiver with remembered desire, made her wince with humiliation. She had never, ever, done anything so stupidly impulsive before. Would never, ever, do anything so stupidly irresponsible again. But, as it turned out, once had been plenty. One chance in a million, and she'd gotten pregnant.

If Jessica hadn't offered her a job at the ranch…

But Jess was a good friend, and true. "Come and stay with me," she'd said the minute Abbie had blurted out her troubles. "I could really use your help in the office. I mean it. You'll be doing me a big favor."

Of course, Abbie knew who was getting the most benefit out of this impromptu visit, and she loved her friend all the more for pretending otherwise. After all, how much office work could there be at a ranch? Especially anything Abbie might know how to do. She was an excellent teacher—well, had been, at any rate. She was also a whiz with math and could fill out a tax form while flipping it like a pancake, but what did she know about hay? Or horses? She wouldn't know one end of a ranch from the other. She knew the Colemans raised Arabians on the Desert Rose, and she knew that particular breed of horse had originated in—*duh*—Arabia. But if she was asked to pick the Arabian out of a horse lineup, she'd be playing the odds and they wouldn't be in her favor.

On top of being a real greenhorn, she couldn't fit into her blue jeans anymore, either, and she'd never in her life worn a pair of cowboy boots. But, bottom line, she had nowhere else to go except her parents' home outside of Little Rock, and since that was out of the question, she'd lug these mismatched suitcases outside and look for a cowboy with a big black truck, who was probably scowling in earnest because she was taking so long to get out there.

When all the misfit suitcases were stacked together on a woefully inadequate foldout rolling wire rack, which had been salvaged from the trash at Miss Amelia's, she dragged them past the attendant, who barely even glanced at her baggage check. Probably figured no self-respecting thief would claim such a motley assortment. Abbie bumped her rickety pile of bags toward the exit, balancing the stack carefully and hoping a kind soul would offer some assistance in getting the bulky bundle through the automatic doors. If she'd been a month further along in her pregnancy, someone probably would have. Or if she'd been a month back, when some of that early pregnancy glow had burnished her cheeks with healthy color and given her sandy-brown hair a saucy bounce, she probably could have gotten a helping hand with nothing more than a smile and a *please, would you mind?* But she was five months along, past the glowing phase of impending motherhood and just rounded enough all over to look chubby. At least, she wasn't waddling yet. Well, she didn't think she was, anyway. Although, for all she knew, her rear end might be swaying like a duck's tail.

She bullied the suitcases through the doorway, all on her own, only to have them tumble into an uncooperative pile just on the other side of the electronic eye, which stopped the doors from closing, which subsequently caused a backup of departing passengers and an unsettling *beep, beep, beep* sound. "Sorry," she apologized to the frowning faces in the doorway behind her. "Sorry."

No one offered to help her gather the luggage. One man stepped over the jumble of suitcases, another edged around, but Abbie finally managed to scoot the cases out of the way and off to the side until she could get them straight again. No small task that, as the paisley suitcase seemed to have lost an essential bit of hardware in the tumble and was no longer completely closed. So where was a man when she needed one?

Ah, but she didn't need one. Wasn't that what this entire flight to Texas was about? Wasn't that why she'd told her parents she was spending the summer at a math and science camp in the Pocono Mountains? Wasn't she here to escape from the men in her life? All of them. The only one she would honestly like to see at this moment was the stranger who'd gotten her into this predicament with his dark good looks and a smile that buckled her knees. And the only reason she'd like to see him was to thumb her nose and tell him she didn't need anything from him. Well, except, maybe, some duct tape.

A glance over her left shoulder didn't reveal any black pickup trucks or scowling ranch hands, and a glance over her right showed nothing more than a cluster of people blocking her view. She knew from past arrivals in Austin on her way to the University of Texas grad school that the airport was always crowded and that trying to find a familiar vehicle among the slow tide of cars, buses, trucks and taxis moving past the building could be a formidable task. In the past, she'd been mainly looking for the bus, but hopefully a black truck would be easy to spot. Especially one accompanied by a cowboy.

Regrouping, she shifted the paisley suitcase to the top of the luggage stack so she could keep its contents safely intact with the weight of her hand. Slinging the shoulder strap of her purse high up on her shoulder, she prepared to tilt the baggage onto the wheels of the wire rack and head out to find Jessica's cousin,

Mac. But just as she braced the rack with her foot, tipped it back on the rollers and pushed it like a baby buggy toward the curb, the crowd thinned and her heart pulled taut in a little clutch of recognition as she saw him. *Him.* He'd been wearing a hat that night, too, and even though she couldn't see his face in full now, the hammering, yammering beat of her heart would allow for no mistakes. It was him. The mysterious stranger. The man of her dreams. The father of her baby.

Oh, great. Of all the times to run into him again, this seemed the worst of all possible moments. Maybe she could duck back inside the building, get a drink, visit the ladies' room and give him time to move along. She didn't want a confrontation here, now. Not when her hair was limp and lackluster and tethered by a rubber band in a holding pattern at the back of her neck. Not when she was wearing stretch pants and a comfortably oversize, albeit somewhat sloppy, shirt of her brother's. Not when she'd put on an old pair of black-framed glasses instead of her contacts. Not when she looked and felt about as sexy as leftover oatmeal.

On the other hand, if she didn't march right up to him right now and demand whatever a pregnant, practically penniless woman demanded from a man whose name she didn't know but whose baby she was carrying, the opportunity might never come again. Then again, back to the other hand, she wasn't exactly in the mood to be humiliated and he looked pretty engrossed in conversation with a tanned, long-legged, skinny and obviously not pregnant blonde.

Perfect, Abbie thought. She'd just waddle right over there and let him get a good side-by-side comparison of her at her dumpy, lumpy, travel-weary worst with the disgustingly slender sun goddess whose smile seemed to have him mesmerized. On second thought, laying claim to his arm and his virility would put a definite crimp in his flirting and that would serve him right. *Hi,* she could say brightly. *Remember me? Graduation party last December? So nice to see you again. What do you think we should name our baby?* Oh, yeah, that would cool the ardor in those dark Arabic eyes but good.

Arabic. Arabian.

Oh, now that was just plain silly. Just because Jessica's family raised Arabian horses and December's mystery man had a slight Arabic ethnicity was hardly a reason to link him to the Colemans. That was like setting out to step over a ditch and then taking a running jump at the Grand Canyon instead. There was no basis, no reason at all to jump to such irrational conclusions. She'd just steer her luggage back into the airport, where the air was cool and conducive to logic. Why, five minutes inside and she'd probably realize he didn't even resemble the man she'd met that night. Not even close. And Jessica's cousin would turn out to be a leathery redhead and all would be well.

The cowboy glanced up. His gaze moved past her and returned with a jerk of recognition. Abbie hadn't known she could move so fast. Her foot shoved the base of the wire rack, a move calculated to get the wheels angled and rolling. Worked beautifully, except for that initial wrench of the castors, which caused the luggage to shift and tumble like an avalanche of untimely disaster. The paisley suitcase flew open on impact and a good deal of Abbie's private life sprawled out across the concrete. She knelt to scoop it out of the public domain, tossing panicked looks at the stranger who was already pushing away from the big black truck he'd been leaning against, moving away from the startled blonde, coming straight toward Abbie.

Black truck. Oh, jeez…

"You?" he demanded without preamble.

Abbie shoved her belongings into the suitcase, uncaring of order or wrinkles or that her hands shook so hard she had to pick up some items twice. "You who?" she said in a strangled voice. "You, uh, must have me mixed up with somebody else." She couldn't look at him, couldn't solidify the supposition with the fact that he was who she thought he was and that she was…*gulp*…who he thought *she* was. "You don't have to help me." Scooping up scattered items with new fervor, she kept her head bent and her face averted. "My, uh, boyfriend is here somewhere, he'll be here to help me any minute now. I can't imagine what held him up in there. He was right behind me. Back there. At the baggage claim. Inside."

"Boyfriend?" His voice cracked the word like a whip.

There was probably some special corner of hell reserved for liars, but Abbie clung to the hope she would be pardoned simply because she was so very bad at lying. *Boyfriend?* Now, that was a stroke of insanity. ‘‘Look, whoever you are,’’ she said in a rush of desperation, ‘‘I’m not who you think I am, so go away.’’

He stooped and stared, pushing up the brim of his hat until his familiar dark eyes were peering at her with all the warmth of polished onyx, trying to catch her in a stray glance. And just the feel of his gaze on her created a hurricane of hot remembrance inside her. She couldn’t look at him and she couldn’t not look at him. The most magical night of her entire life had been spent with this man, wrapped in his arms, clothed in his smile, naked in his bed…on the floor, the chair, the vanity… Abbie wrestled the memory into submission. She didn’t want to deny the experience, but she was scared to death to claim it, too. What if the blonde was his wife? What if he *had* mistaken Abbie for someone else? What if he thought she’d stolen his wallet or something? What if he believed they’d met at a bar mitzvah instead of at the street dance? What if he kissed her? Right here, right now? He was still staring at her and she struggled to locate a tone of offence. ‘‘You have mistaken me for someone else,’’ she pronounced defiantly.

‘‘No,’’ he said coldly. ‘‘It’s *you,* all right.’’

Abbie swallowed hard, willed him to move on, get along, disappear, as she lifted her chin with completely false bravado. ‘‘Well, I don’t know you, even if you are standing on my underwear.’’

He was, too. And of course, it had to be a pair of her serviceable, sedate and completely unattractive maternity underpants. They were new, but that was about the most complimentary thing anyone could say about them.

He seemed stuck for words as he stared at the scrap of unimaginative white peeking out from beneath his boot. So Abbie gave another verbal nudge to shoo him on his way. ‘‘Would you mind moving your big foot?’’

With an economy of movements he scooped up the panties without even looking at them and let them dangle, without dignity, on the end of his index finger. ‘‘With my compliments,’’ he said.

Abbie snatched the lingerie and stuffed it into the mangled suitcase. ‘‘Yes, well, thanks. Hope you find whoever it is you're looking for.’’

He shrugged, straightened and turned to walk away. Abbie knew she was a fool to let him go without a word. She owed him an explanation. Well, at least, she owed him the knowledge of his impending fatherhood. If she'd never seen him again, she could have lived with knowing she'd had no chance to tell him. She could have found a way of explaining to their child that one parent would always remain a mystery. But now he was here and he deserved to know, whether or not she wanted to tell him.

Gathering the rest of her scattered belongings, she closed the suitcase as best she could and stood straight, holding it tightly in her arms. She'd just stack the luggage on the rack, get it out of the way, then she'd walk over and admit she was indeed the *you* he'd thought she was. With a glance, she noted the well-formed shape of his backside and remembered vividly the way that same backside had looked without tight-fitting jeans. She jerked her gaze from the hip pockets of his Levi's and checked to see if the blonde was still there. She was. As was the truck. The big, black truck with the emblem of a horse's head stamped on the side. A horse head with full Arabian show gear—horse savvy or not, Abbie recognized the regalia—and, in case she hadn't, the words *Desert Rose* circled across the top and *Arabians* looped up from the bottom.

Oh, no! This couldn't be happening. Couldn't be true. Fate wouldn't play this kind of joke on her. The mystery man couldn't be Jessica Coleman's cousin. That would be too—she couldn't even think of a word to describe how perfectly awful that would be. It didn't help to think the sequence of events made an odd sort of sense now, either. The party after the graduation she'd shared with Jessica, about three hundred other grad students and whoever else had shown up to help celebrate, the fact that both their families were there, but somehow, in all the fanfare and folderol, none of the Colemans had gotten introduced to any of the Joneses. The way she'd met the mystery man at the outdoor, portable bar moments after Jessica had mentioned her cousin had gone to get a drink. It was all so impossible, and yet suddenly so completely plausible that Abbie forced her gaze up from the Desert Rose crest to the face of the man she now knew without a doubt was here to pick her up. Could this situation be any more embarrassing?

"Mac," she whispered aloud, because she had to feel the shape of his name in her mouth, had to affirm that he was both mystery man and Jessica's cousin, had to do something to keep from melting into a puddle of humiliation right there on the hot Austin airport pavement.

He couldn't have heard her whisper. Yet he turned, nevertheless, still questioning her presence, her identity, her denials. But one look at her ashen face must have told the story. His gaze tracked hers to the Desert Rose insignia on the door of the truck and then returned with a flare of comprehension. His chin came up as he tugged the brim of his hat down to shade his eyes, and she noted, as if from a great distance, that his shoulders were moving up and down, up and down, in coordination with the rapid expansion of his chest as he inhaled, exhaled, inhaled.

It was a loud moment, unique in that while she was incapable of hearing anything except the frantic flutter of her own breath rasping like a bellows from her lungs, she absorbed the noise of traffic, of planes taking off overhead, of voices all around, of arrivals and welcomes, and car engines starting, revving, receding. She listened, though, only to the echoes of his voice in her mind and knew he was grappling with the same set of impossible, improbable, implacable chain of events she'd just worked her way through. She knew, too, the instant he reached the same inevitable conclusion.

''Abbie?'' His voice was incredulous, hesitant with dismay, rough with amazement. ''Are you Abbie?''

Chapter Two

Mac's boots might as well have fused with the hot pavement for all his ability to move them. He couldn't seem to do anything except stare at Abigail Jones, his mystery date, his cousin's friend, the woman he'd come to the airport to meet. How was it that fate had turned aside every attempt he'd made in the past five months to discover who she was only to unaccountably drop her back into his life at this precise instant? Why had she denied knowing him when he remembered her so vividly? How could she have forgotten him when his whole body held the memory of hers?

She looked the same, but different, too. She'd worn a short, slender, sensational dress the night they'd met—except for later, when she'd worn nothing at all—and now she was dressed in a baggy shirt that was too big for her by half, but which made her look small and absurdly sexy. She might be a little more filled out than before, but that could just be the clothes and the way her hair was pulled back at her nape instead of curling loosely about her shoulders as it had that night. The glasses were definitely new, though.

She must have been wearing contacts when they'd met. Or maybe she hadn't needed glasses then. Or maybe she had but hadn't gotten them yet. What if she hadn't seen him clearly at all that night, and that was why she claimed she didn't recognize him now? Except she had recognized him. Her bowed head, the way she wouldn't meet his gaze, the breathy, scattered tones of her voice all belied her spoken doubt. He'd have known her anywhere, anytime...the eyes as blue as Texas bluebonnets, hair not quite blond, not quite brown, but a soft, honeyed shade in between; the slight upward tilt at the end of her nose; the deceptively demure lift of her chin; the set of her shoulders; the warm tones of her skin. In that one glimpse, memory had flooded his mind's eye with images of her. His body, too, remembered, and he'd known her as much by the physical response as by sight.

Jessica must have set this up somehow. But how could she have known he and Abbie had ever met? He hadn't even made the connection until just now. And Abbie looked equally astonished. Appalled, even, as she stood there, clasping a dilapidated suitcase in her arms and staring at him as if he were the ghost of Christmas Yet to Come. He was surprised to see her, but not shaken, as she appeared to be. She'd said there was a boyfriend with her, which had made Mac unaccountably angry. But there was still no sign of another man, and Jess certainly was expecting only one guest. Mac figured any significant other of Abbie's was a long way from here, or invented on the spot to save embarrassment.

But whether or not there was a boyfriend, Abbie had been traveling and she obviously needed help with her luggage. Mac couldn't just keep standing there, stuck in the moment, awash in unaccustomed emotion, wondering how he could keep from scaring her away again, wondering if it was all right to admit he was glad—so glad—to see her again.

"Hey, remember me?" said a voice near his ear. The leggy blonde, who'd been in the process of inviting him to spend some quality time with her at the Four Seasons. Betsy or Bambi or whatever the hell she'd said her name was had been completely forgotten the moment his gaze had fallen on Abbie. *Abbie. Abigail Jones.* What a plain and glorious name. How well it suited her, too. He wanted to say it over and over. He wanted to welcome her back into his life with a kiss. Oh, yeah, he especially wanted to kiss her. But his knees were stupidly weak and his heart was beating ridiculously fast and she was just standing there staring at him as someone tugged at his elbow, demanded his attention.

"What's the matter?" the blonde asked. "Is the heat getting to you? You were about to offer me a ride, remember?"

"I was?" He couldn't take his eyes off Abbie, who continued to clutch the one suitcase with its wispy flags of underwear peeking out around the edges, as she trundled the whole rickety stack of luggage toward him. He stepped out, offering in a gesture to take the suitcase from her arms, but she stopped like a skittish filly at his first advance and eyed him nervously.

"You're Mac?" Her voice was a shaky whisper, and he edged closer to hear her.

"Mac Coleman," he said, as if they needed an introduction. "I'm Jessica's cousin."

"I was afraid you were going to say that." Abbie wrinkled her nose, then tried to adjust her glasses via facial contortions because her hands were wrapped around the broken suitcase, and, for some reason, she didn't seem to want to let go. "Holy Maloney, this is awkward."

"Doesn't need to be." He put his hands on the suitcase, wanting to be gallant and charming and helpful, but when he gave the bag a tug, she clasped it all the tighter. "I can show you Jess's picture in my wallet," he offered, "if it'll reassure you and make you feel more at ease. She really wanted to come in to meet you today, but there's a lot of work at the ranch, what with my brothers getting married recently and not spending as much time helping as usual, and I had business in town today anyway, so here we are." He was talking too much, trying too hard, wanting quite desperately to see her smile.

She sighed instead. "This is really awkward."

"And here I am, thinking that seeing you again is such a pleasant surprise."

"Yes, well, you haven't seen that much of me yet." She glanced at the other woman, licked her lips, pressed them together, and Mac, interpreting the glance as anxiety, hurried to reassure her.

"She was just asking me where she could catch the hotel shuttle," he said, gesturing dismissively at the blonde, never transferring his full—and hopefully charming—attention from Abbie. ''How have you been since...December?''

Her blue eyes shifted doubtfully to him. She opened her mouth, closed it again, then sucked in a deep breath, squared her shoulders and said in a rush, ''Pregnant. How have you been?''

His smile faded, along with the excitement and possibility that seeing her again had evoked. *Pregnant?* What had she said? ''Pregnant?'' he repeated, his gut clenching in protest as his gaze dropped helplessly to her midsection.

''Pregnant,'' she confirmed, thrusting the suitcase at him and revealing the unmistakably rounded contours of her belly beneath the oversize white shirt. ''Congratulations, it's yours.''

ABBIE COULDN'T BELIEVE she'd just blurted it out that way. But then, there probably wasn't a good way to tell a complete stranger you were having his baby. Miss Manners ought to put together a pamphlet of suggestions. Mac's expression was turning grimmer by the second, but oddly enough, Abbie felt a certain amount of relief. It had been a strain to keep the secret and now, whether for better or worse, it was out of the bag. She turned her attention to the other woman, who was eyeing her with a curious hostility. ''Hi,'' she said, offering a handshake with her now unencumbered hand. ''I'm Abbie Jones. I'm sorry to have interrupted. I know this must seem a little strange.''

''This is Bambi.'' Mac's voice had all the warmth of a refrigerator as he butted in to make the introduction. "We're giving her a ride to her hotel before we head out to the ranch."

"Brandi," the blonde corrected amiably. "But maybe I should go look for that shuttle and let you two work out your...problem."

But Mac—pale beneath his dark skin—stayed her with a glance. "No. Please," he requested in a voice no one in their right mind would argue with. "I want to give you a ride to the hotel. It will be my pleasure. Once her—" he jerked his head toward Abbie "—*boyfriend* gets out here, we'll be ready to roll and as friendly as four coyotes on a foggy day."

"There's no boyfriend," Abbie admitted in a rush, determined to be truthful from here on in. "You startled me and I...well, I just made him up for protection. Before I knew we were going to have to get better acquainted."

Mac looked at her, clearly unimpressed with the truth. "Get in," he said.

Abbie didn't know how this could work out, but she wasn't getting into that truck, and she didn't really think Brandi should do so, either. "I'm not going to the ranch," she announced with more gusto than guts. "Not now."

Mac tossed her suitcase into the back of the truck and reached for another, his gaze dropping to her rounded waistline and skittering quickly away. "You're going to the ranch. Jess is expecting you. She's expecting me to get you there safe and sound. You're going."

Abbie raised her chin. "I'm not."

The red plaid suitcase landed in the pickup bed,

and was quickly followed by the duct-taped brown tweed. "Yes," he said, "you are."

"I can get a cab." Brandi edged toward the curb, but Mac touched her arm and his voice warmed. "I want to take you to the hotel. So, please. Get in the truck."

Brandi looked at Abbie, assessing perhaps the odds of getting caught in the middle of a lovers' quarrel against the odds of getting a cab against the odds that this awkward situation might be resolved in her favor. Her glance skipped to the Desert Rose insignia on the truck, flickered over Abbie's tousled appearance and then returned to Mac, accompanied by a beatific smile. "Well, if you're sure it's no trouble."

"No trouble at all." Although anyone listening might have thought otherwise. "Happy to do it."

He wasn't happy about anything, Abbie thought, as she watched him toss in the last suitcase, uncaring as to where—or even if—it landed. Okay, so she'd give him the benefit of the doubt. Anger was a perfectly understandable first reaction. Impending parenthood wasn't always welcome news, even under far better circumstances than this. He hadn't, obviously, been expecting to see her ever again, had been as surprised by her as she had been by him. Even without the pregnancy, he might be forgiven a lack of excitement at seeing her. He had, after all, been flirting rather successfully with beautiful Brandi before Abbie appeared and put his agenda on the skids. Well, thinking she had done anything more than delay the outcome of his flirtation was probably stretching it, considering that Brandi was sitting pretty in the middle of the truck's bench seat at this very moment.

Still, Abbie didn't see how any good could come from letting a darkly handsome Texan tell her what to do. He'd been her accomplice in getting into this sorry situation in the first place and that was quite enough help, thank you very much. "I'm not going with you," she said firmly. "Take my bags out of the back of the truck right now so I can put them on the first plane out of here."

He looked at her across the expanse of pickup bed and luggage. "Too late for second thoughts, Abigail. If you hadn't wanted to stake your claim on me, you wouldn't have come here in the first place. Now, get in and let's go."

"Stake a claim?" Abbie repeated, not certain she'd heard him correctly. "What does that mean? You think I knew you and Jessie were cousins? Is that what you're saying?"

He shrugged. "If the shoe fits..."

"Well, that's insane. If I'd known you were Jessica's cousin, you'd better believe I'd be anywhere but here."

"Easy enough to say now that you are here. But regardless of what I believe to be true and not true, I'm taking you to the ranch. Jessica wants you there and I'm not going to be the one to explain to her why you've suddenly changed your mind. Now, get in and let's go as *planned.*" He stressed the word, making it sound ominous and threatening.

"You can't force me to go with you."

"The hell I can't. You've just accused me of being

the father of your baby. I think that gives me a little say in where you go from here. Cut to the chase, Abigail Jones. The Desert Rose has been your destination for months. There's no good reason to balk now, when you're so close to your goal.''

Oh, he was arrogant. And maddening. And sure of himself. And wrong, wrong, wrong. He was also so handsome it made her chest hurt. ''Fine,'' she said, mainly because her choices at the moment were extremely limited and because she was weary all the way to the roots of her hair. ''But I'm not staying.''

He just looked at her, coolly disbelieving. ''Your display of reluctance is duly noted. Now, get in.'' Then he got in on the driver's side and started the engine.

Abbie debated her options and decided that kicking truck tires would be about as pointless as any other show of defiance. She thought about climbing into the back of the pickup and tossing out her luggage as haphazardly as he'd tossed it in. She could be in Dallas in an hour, in Little Rock an hour after that. But now that she knew who he was, now that she'd told him the truth, sooner or later, in one place or another, she'd have to face him again. And now was as good a time as any. He was a jerk, but he might as well learn straight away that she was no coward.

She scooted in beside Brandi and slammed the door.

''...AND WOULDN'T YOU KNOW IT? Right in the middle of the presentation, the thing breaks and all my careful planning vanishes as quickly as the available balance on my credit card!''

Mac changed gears and merged into the lane of traffic while bubbly Brandi filled the stilted atmosphere inside the truck with chatter. He wished he hadn't insisted she come with them, wished he'd never pretended an interest in her at all, wished he could yell mightily at Abbie, who was all but hugging the passenger side door in a wretched silence. Not that she deserved even the slightest hint of his compassion. She'd set him up, dammit. Laid her trap so cleverly he'd practically begged to walk into it.

A baby.

Well, it wasn't his baby, that was for sure. No way in hell was she going to pin this on him. No, sir. Uh-uh. No two ways about it. She'd already admitted she was a liar. Claiming there was a boyfriend with her at the airport. Ha! That had been her first mistake.

No, choosing him as her target had been her first mistake. He was no gullible Gus, ready to accept her claim as truth, her accusations for fact. She was grasping at straws if she believed he was so easily duped. He knew what she was after—the Coleman name, the Desert Rose ranch, the royal heritage of a lost prince of Arabia. Most likely Jessica had been manipulated into filling in all the blank spaces of his life that Abbie hadn't been able to ferret out on her own. No doubt, Abbie knew the story of his past as well as he did, himself. He wouldn't be surprised to discover she had a scrapbook containing all the newspaper clippings that made up his history—Rose Coleman's storybook wedding to Ibrahim El Jeved, the crown prince of

Sorajhee. The birth of a son, Alim, now called Alex. The birth of twins, Makin and Kadar, whose names were later changed to Mac and Cade. Ibrahim's murder. Rose's banishment and reported death. The rescue of three young princes by their uncle. The success of the Coleman-Grayson business partnership. The prime Arabian stock bred and trained on the Desert Rose. The secrecy, the speculation, the scandals of the royal family of El Jeved.

Mac figured Abbie knew it all, right down to the last decimal point in his personal bank account. Oh, yeah. She'd snowed Jessica, somehow, and gotten close enough to find out all she needed to know to seduce him. Sweet, innocent little Abbie had a calculating heart and a devious agenda. Well, he'd be damned if he'd give her even a penny for her trouble, much less his name and heritage. It wasn't his baby. It couldn't be his. One night? A million-to-one chance? No. No. She didn't deserve the benefit of the doubt. He knew her type, had been badly burned before, and it was not a lesson he had any intention of repeating.

He should have made her find her own way out to the ranch. But some masochistic impulse had made him order her to get into his truck, had urged him to punish himself at the same time he let her know, in no uncertain terms, that he was nobody's fool. Chances are, though, even had he tried to send her on her way, she'd have beaten him home. Women like her always had a backup plan.

"Even the best-laid plans can't guarantee success,"

he said pointedly, for Abbie's benefit. "Sometimes a scheme is doomed from the inception."

"My, my, don't you have a cynical attitude," Brandi observed in cheery tones as she rubbed her shoulder against his arm. "But, as it turned out, I still managed to snag the account. There's more than one way to get a man to say yes. Isn't that right, Abbie?"

Abbie raised her head and for a second, her eyes locked with Mac's before she turned away. "Frankly, I've never thought a man was worth that much effort."

Brandi laughed and blithely continued on with her chatter while Abbie returned to staring out the window and Mac fumed over her haughty tone of voice. She had no business taking the offensive like that, sounding wounded, somehow, in spite of the sting in her words. He heartily wished he'd left both women on the curb at the airport. "Four Seasons hotel," he said, relieved to see the hotel come into view.

"So soon?" Brandi lurched forward to see, jostling Abbie in the process.

Mac wanted to grab her arm and tell her to be more careful. Abbie was pregnant, for Pete's sake. But then he had no right or reason to think Abbie needed his protection. Or to give it, if she did. Truth be told, he should be thanking Brandi for providing him the protection of her chatter this far. "I'll walk you in," he said, as he parked in a No Parking space in front of the hotel, opened the door and stepped out.

Brandi slid out of the seat after him, not offering so much as a glance at Abbie, much less a word of goodbye, chattering instead to Mac like some silly magpie.

Abbie was the one who said a warm "nice to have met you," even though she'd been mainly ignored throughout the trip. Mac felt irritated by one woman's lack of manners and by the other one's innate courtesy. And on top of it, he recognized a strong thrust of concern at the weary note that echoed in Abbie's voice. Probably part of her act, a link in the plan to claim his future for herself and her baby. Well, she'd find it rough going. He had experience with women like her and their end-justifies-the-means attitude. It'd be a cold day in the Sahara before he set himself up to play the fool again.

When he got back into the truck cab, a full twenty minutes had elapsed. Most of it while he stood inside the lobby listening to Brandi as she did her best to persuade him to return later for cocktails, dinner and a late-night dessert in her room, but mainly while he watched the truck, making sure Abbie didn't get out and signal for a cab. He didn't know why he should care if she did. The sooner she figured out her little plan had run smack into the proverbial mountain, the better off both of them would be.

"I didn't much figure you'd have the good sense to slip away when I gave you the chance," he said, turning the key in the ignition. "Your kind never does."

"My *kind,* as you put it, does better at escaping when *your* kind leaves the keys in the truck." Anger flashed in her eyes and he met it with cool deliberation. "Besides, if you were so anxious for me to leave, why didn't you let me go at the airport instead of dragging me all the way into town?"

"I was only trying to be accommodating."

"You were demonstrating to me that responsibility isn't your forte. Fine, I got the message. Now, take me back to the airport and I'll be out of your life for good."

"If it wasn't for Jessica, I'd do just that and call your bluff, but good."

She looked down at her stomach. "You think this is a bluff?"

Easing the pickup into the flow of traffic that was always heavy in downtown Austin, he felt the sting of her righteous—now, there was a misnomer—anger and smiled lazily. "You'll find I'm not one to mince words," he said. "And I don't take kindly to being accused of something I didn't do."

"What are you saying?" Abbie asked tightly. "That perhaps you have an identical twin who was in that hotel room with us last December and at the moment of conception it was him instead of you?"

Mac shot her an irritated glance. "As it happens, I do have a twin brother. Cade. But as we both know, he's no more the father of that baby you're carrying than I am."

She blinked, then adjusted her glasses with a jab of her finger. "You mean you really do have a twin? For real?"

"Don't play games. You probably know more about me and my family than I do."

"I don't see how you can say that. Until I saw you outside the airport, I didn't even know your name."

He clicked his tongue disapprovingly. "The more lies you tell, the more apt you are to get caught in them," he admonished. "You and Jessica became friends during grad school. Don't try to tell me you never talked about your families."

"I suppose someone of your kind would find it impossible to believe you weren't the main topic of conversation every day of the week, every hour of the day, but believe me, stranger things have happened."

"Yes, like you showing up here."

"I'm here because Jessica was kind enough to invite me. As I said before, if I'd known you were one of her cousins, this is the last place I'd have chosen as a refuge."

"Refuge? Now, that's an interesting turn of phrase."

She pressed her lips together and stared stonily out the windshield. "Look, Mac—it is all right if I call you Mac, isn't it?"

"I usually require women to call me Sheikh Makin Bin Habib El Jeved, or Prince, but since you asked so nicely, I'll make an exception for you and allow you to call me Your Royal Highness." He slowed in response to the traffic and looked over at her. "I'm guessing my connection to the royal family of Sorajhee doesn't come as a surprise to you."

Her blue eyes took on something of a glaze at that. "Oh, no. I'm not surprised at all. I was sort of hoping for Prince William—he's young, but so handsome, you know—but what kind of commoner am I to complain? I mean, any royal blood is better than none, right?"

She was making fun of him, the little witch. There was a hint of a dimple winking at him from her cheek, the dance of devilment in her eyes. She was laughing, and his stupid heart urged him to laugh with her! But he would not give her the satisfaction. He would never humble himself in that way. "I'm glad you find it so amusing," he said stiffly. "You may not find it so in the days to come."

"Day," she corrected quickly. "I'm not staying any longer than it takes to convince Jessica I'll be okay somewhere else."

"Some other place of refuge?"

"I didn't mean to say that. Refuge sounds...well, not the way it really is."

"So how is it, Abigail Jones? Did you get into trouble and this looked like an easy way out? Or was this your plan all along?"

The laughter went out of her expression as quickly as a room goes from light to dark with the flick of a switch. "My *plan* was to take my graduate degree and teach. My *plan* was to be on my own and independent. My *plan* was to stay out of trouble altogether. I didn't *plan* to get pregnant, I didn't *plan* on ever seeing you again, and I sure as shootin' didn't *plan* to answer stupid questions about looking for the easy way out!"

Mac thought she sounded genuinely upset. Angry, too. He had to admit she was a consummate little actress. "Let's be honest, Abbie. We had one night together. One. We weren't careless. We used protection. You'll forgive me if I refuse to believe I'm the father of your child."

She was furious. It showed in every nuance, in every movement, in the white-hot gaze that scorched him in its outrage. "And you'll forgive me if I believe you're a jackass."

"There's no need to resort to name-calling."

"No, much better to stick to your civilized way of calling me not only a liar, but a wh—"

"I did not say that."

"But you did imply it." She twisted irritably on the seat. "Well, I don't care what you believe, Mr. Sheikh El Highness, but for your information, I *don't* sleep around, using *protection* is no guarantee against pregnancy, and this *is* your baby. Much to my regret. Now, please, don't talk to me anymore. No," she snapped when he opened his mouth. "Don't say another word. I'm dangerously hormonal and I might start screaming. I might dial 911 on my cell phone and accuse you of kidnapping. Or worse. I might take out a pair of needles and start knitting little booties. Believe me, you'll be doing us both a favor if you keep quiet from here on in and just concentrate on driving."

Mac thought maybe—this time, anyway—she had a valid point.

Chapter Three

"I've been so excited all day, I barely got anything done." Jessica led the way up the broad, curving staircase to the second floor, chattering away as she tossed speculative glances over her shoulder at Abbie, who trailed after her like a shadow with flushed cheeks and black-framed glasses. Something was wrong with this picture, Jessica had decided within two minutes of her friend's arrival. Something more than the awkwardness of her circumstances had put those high points of color into Abbie's cheeks and given her chin its stubborn tilt. She'd practically fallen out of the truck in her haste to meet Jess's enthusiastic welcome, an action that could have been an indication of tremendous gratitude or an eagerness to get out of range of Mac's formidable frown.

Jess had caught a glimpse of it, purely by chance, and her curiosity had spiked with the possibility that one thing had something to do with the other. Of course, it could be sheer happenstance that Mac's brow was furrowed with thunderclouds and Abbie's blue eyes seemed unnecessarily dark and stormy. There were probably any number of logical explanations, Jessica thought, although none occurred readily to her. Abbie looked like someone had popped her balloon, taken away her candy, made her drop her ice cream and left her plenty mad in the process.

Jessica pondered the possibilities on the trek up the stairs and maintained a bright stream of conversation to disguise it. "You'll be in here," she said, opening the door of the guest bedroom. "Mom and Dad have the master suite down the hall and my bedroom adjoins yours on the other side. It'll be almost like being back at the grad house."

"Except for sharing the bathroom with six other women," Abbie said, her smile never quite reaching her eyes.

"And the raucous fraternity parties across the street," Jessica added. "Mac is still living across the hall." She indicated the suite of rooms on the other side of the stairs. "But he's normally pretty quiet. He's gone a lot, too, to horse shows and auctions and stuff. I accuse him of being lonely now that Cade is married and living in one of the guest houses with Serena. You did know Mac has an identical twin, didn't you?"

"He mentioned it on the trip out," Abby said in a voice just shy of snippy.

"There was quite a stir last month when Cade went off to Balahar pretending to be Mac and accidentally married King Zakariyya Al Farid's adopted daughter and then wound up falling hard for her. Cade and Serena got remarried because they weren't sure the first ceremony was legal in the States, since they'd used Mac's name instead of Cade's during the ceremony in Balahar. It was a big mess for a while there, but all's well that ends well, you know.'' Jessica stood aside and motioned Abbie into the bedroom. ''Did I ever tell you that my cousins are really from a country called Sorajhee on the edge of Saudi Arabia?''

Abbie stopped abruptly, only a step inside the room. ''I thought he was making that up. You mean, he's not really American? Not really a Texan?''

''Don't let any one of them hear you say that. They're Texans through and through,'' Jessica said with a laugh. ''They've always had dual citizenship because their mother, my aunt Rose, didn't give up her citizenship when she married the crown prince of Sorajhee. It was a big scandal in their country at the time, but she became a beloved queen in spite of it. Then when King Ibrahim was murdered, Aunt Rose believed her sons were in danger and got my dad to help smuggle the three boys out of the country and that's how they ended up as Colemans in Bridle, Texas. It's quite a story, but I won't drown you in the family history—as interesting as it is—until you've been here at least long enough to unpack your bags.''

Abbie sank onto the edge of the bed as if her legs weren't strong enough to support her. ''You mean, he's really a...a *prince?*''

''Mac?'' Aha, Jessica thought, pretending to take no notice that of the three male cousins, Abbie had twice now referred only to one. Of course, she had yet to meet Alex and Cade, and she had just spent the long ride from the airport to the ranch alone with

Mac, but still… ''Prince of aggravation, if you want my true opinion,'' Jess said with an affectionate laugh. ''They came to live with Mom and Dad before I was even born, so they're more like brothers than cousins and Mac is the worst when it comes to teasing me. When he really wants to get me riled, he calls me 'Husky' because that breed of dog often has eyes that are different colored and he knows how much I hate having one blue eye and one green one. When he just wants to agitate me a little, he calls me Blondie.'' She touched her carroty red hair, wishing it was blond or black, or even a nice sandy-brown like Abbie's.

Abbie offered a small smile, but it was obvious her thoughts were elsewhere.

''Well, listen to me, nattering at you about my cousins, when it's clear you need a chance to catch your breath and get your bearings. I don't know what's keeping Mac.'' She glanced over her shoulder in time to see him clear the landing and stalk down the hall towards the guest room, a bag under each arm and one in each hand. His whole expression was as dark as a Texas tornado and Jessica couldn't keep her eyebrows from arching in sharpening suspicion. As curious as it seemed, something unpleasant must have happened between her cousin and her friend on the trip out from Austin.

''You want to be in or out?'' he asked, his tone of voice as tight and short as the check rein on a green colt. ''I can't get all these bags through the doorway with you standing in it.''

Jessica stepped farther into the room, clearing the

doorway for him and his temper. He took two long strides into the room and dumped all four suitcases onto the bed. "Miss Jones. Jessica," he said, acknowledging and dismissing their presence in three cool-as-icicles words. Then, without a glance at Abbie, who was now surrounded by a motley assortment of luggage, he strode out of the room as if somebody had insulted every single one of his prize Arabians. The thud of his boot heels on the stairs echoed with military precision and then, in final salute to his dark mood, the front door slammed behind him.

Jessie blinked. She'd never seen Mac act that way before. He could be as charming as a patch of bluebells in the spring, or as haughty as Jabbar, the Desert Rose foundation sire, a black Arabian stallion who, on occasion, took his status as champion entirely too seriously. But she'd never seen Mac be rude to anyone and especially not to a female. And one of her good friends, at that. Her gaze swung back to Abbie as suspicion crystallized and ran rampant in her thoughts. What could have caused the two of them to take such an instant dislike to the other? Could Abbie have inadvertently said something to set off an exchange of words? Maybe Mac had uttered some ill-advised statement. But they'd only just met. What could possibly have caused a rift of this magnitude in a drive of barely an hour?

Filing away her questions, Jessie indicated the adjoining bath with a gesture. "There's the bath. It opens into my room on the other side, so just lock that door when you go in, and don't forget to unlock it when you leave. I'll get out of here and let you rest a little while before dinner. Unpack or take a nap or a shower, or whatever you feel like doing. I'll be downstairs in the office, if you need anything or when you're ready for the grand tour. Dinner's at six. We're pretty casual, although Mom has been known to check for dirt on the knuckles or behind the ears, so be forewarned.''

''I'll be sure and wash my ears, then,'' Abbie said, trying for a smile but looking mainly mad and scared and like the smallest gust of wind would send her tumbling backward into the pile of suitcases. ''Hands, too.''

''Mom will be pleased. She's looking forward to meeting you, as is everyone. I've talked about you so much and they're all excited that you're going to help out in the office. I'm so happy you're here, Abbie. And so glad you felt you could call me when you lost your job. I hope you'll feel right at home here at the Desert Rose and I want you to stay as long as you want.''

Abbie's smile quavered even more at that. ''I don't know, Jessie.''

''Don't feel you have to give us any time frame at all. I mean it. You're doing me such a favor by helping out. I've been buried in paperwork the last couple of months and still it keeps pouring in! You may run away screaming when you see my desk. It's just awful.'' Jess knew she was blathering on and on, but the atmosphere was charged somehow with an element she couldn't put her finger on or identify. ''I haven't told anyone except Mom and Aunt Rose about your being pregnant and losing your job and needing a place to get your thoughts together, so don't feel as if you need to explain anything to anyone. Not even me."

"Not much to tell." Abbie stood and smoothed the shirt over her belly to reveal the firm roundness of it. "I haven't even told my parents yet, and look at me. Already as ripe as a June melon." She sighed. "I'm in such a mess, Jessie, and I'm grateful beyond words that you invited me here, but I just don't think I can stay. Not now."

"You're staying," Jessica said firmly. "And if Mac said anything to upset you, I'll wring his neck in three places."

Abbie's eyes went wide with panic. "No, please, don't. I mean, why would you think he upset me?"

Bingo, Jess thought, although she still couldn't quite tally the clues into a clear and likely conclusion. "Well, no more talk about not staying, then. Get unpacked and don't worry about a thing. I mean it! You need a couple of weeks to get your thoughts together and decide what you want to do. This is the perfect place. No one will bother you, I promise. Well, that's not entirely true. I'll probably pester you to death with office work, but other than that, you'll have plenty of time to rest and make a few decisions. Then, when the moment comes to tell your folks, you'll know what you want to say." She smiled broadly. "Now, telling your brothers may be a different story, if they're as zealously overprotective as you've said they are."

"Whatever I told you about them was an understatement," Abbie said with a rueful sigh. "They're going to drive me crazy with their ideas on what I need to do and when, where, how, and why I need to do it. I'm really, really, *really* dreading the moment they have to know.''

''Well, for now, at least, you'll have some peace and quiet so you can make your own decisions before you have to face them.''

''I just hope they don't find me in the meantime.'' Abbie opened her purse and pulled out a compact cell phone. ''I'm going to use this phone whenever I call home and even then, I'm going to be very careful about what I say. On the off chance they call you, just tell them that as far as you know, I'm spending the summer at a math and science camp in the Catskills.''

''If that's your story, I'll stick to it until you tell me otherwise.'' Jess couldn't help it. She gave Abbie a hug. ''This is going to work out great for both of us, Abbie. Everything will turn out for the best, I just know it. Now I'm really getting out of here and giving you some time to settle in.'' Bouncing on her heels, she grinned at Abbie and walked to the door, looking back to see if her friend's expression was in any degree lighter. It was. In fact, Abbie was looking around the room as if she couldn't imagine a nicer place to call her temporary home. ''And on the off chance Mac did say something stupid on the drive out, don't take it personally,'' Jessie cautioned. ''He's just been in a very black mood for the past few months.''

Abbie looked up, startled into a revealing expression. ''Mac didn't say anything,'' she declared, too quickly to be believable. ‘‘Please don’t mention to him that you thought he had.’’

‘‘Sure thing. There’s soap and extra towels in the armoire by the bathroom door. Anything else you need, just ask. And thanks, Abbie, for coming. It means a lot to me to have you here.’’ She stepped into the hall and closed the door behind her before Abbie felt obligated to reply. Jessie couldn’t imagine what had happened between her cousin and her friend, but she was determined to get to the bottom of it by noon tomorrow—or give Mac a major headache in the attempt.

MAC SLAMMED THE DOOR of his pickup, unable to vent the depth of his frustration no matter how many doors he slammed. He’d avoided Abigail Jones and her crass accusations by avoiding everyone. He’d dumped her bags in the guest room, slammed the front door behind him and hightailed it off the ranch. He wanted nothing to do with her and didn’t trust himself to stay away from her, so he climbed right back into his pickup—slamming the door so hard, he was surprised the window didn’t break—and drove off without a word to anyone.

He’d driven with a scowl all the way into Fredericksburg, where he’d ordered a dinner he didn’t eat and a beer he didn’t drink, and stared out the restaurant window until the waiter asked for the umpteenth time if everything was satisfactory, to which Mac had replied finally ‘‘No. No, it isn’t.’’ Then he’d thrown who knows how much money onto the table to make up for not touching the food and drink and walked out, every bit as miserable as when he'd walked in. Driving west to San Marcos, he'd stopped to skip rocks into the muddy Blanco River, then slammed the pickup door once again and driven a succession of winding roads back to Bridle and the ranch, a round trip of close to two hundred miles. And all he'd accomplished was to shift his mood from black to gloomy gray.

He figured Abbie had told her lies to the whole family by now, and his absence had only given them validity. But what did he care? His family would stand shoulder to shoulder with him when they knew the truth. He could count on them. If there was anything in life he was certain of, it was that family mattered. Right now, they might all be wondering why he'd allowed Abbie to lure him into the same trap Gillian had set for him only a couple of years before. On the other hand, they might have greeted Abbie's tale of woe with a sympathetic ear. But once he revealed her for the fraud she was, his family would stand with him against her. He knew they would.

Of course, it probably would have made things easier for them if he'd stood his ground tonight instead of running like a coward who had something to hide. But he just couldn't bear the thought of sitting across the dinner table from the woman who'd haunted his dreams for months now, knowing her for the schemer she obviously had been all along. So he ran. Running from the memory of Gillian's betrayal two years ago. Running from the memory of how sweet Abbie's kiss had seemed five months earlier. Running from his own traitorous heart, which couldn't seem to distinguish between lust and love. It was nearly midnight now and for all the miles he'd gone, he hadn't outrun even one of the voices in his head. *Gillian had lied to him. Abbie had lied to him. Women could not be trusted. There wasn't an ounce of honor among them.*

Okay, so there were a few good ones out there. His two new sisters-in-law, Hannah and Serena, for example. Neither of them would have considered resorting to trickery and treachery to gain the name of Coleman. He couldn't imagine them staking the life of a child against the possibility of an advantageous marriage, as Gillian had done. As Abbie was doing. His cousin, too, was as moral and honest as any old-fashioned girl, but then Jessie was born a Coleman and had been raised with the proper respect for the truth. Olivia Smith, the young ranch hand he'd taken on as an assistant trainer, was as wholesome as fresh butter and far too good with horses to harbor any deceit. Horses, especially Arabians, had a keen sense of just who could be trusted and who couldn't. Then, on the list of honorable women, there was Aunt Vi, who couldn't even tell a fib without blushing a vivid, culpable red. And although Mac had only recently begun to know his mother, Rose, he refused to believe she had ever stooped to duplicity when it came to dealing with his father, or any other man.

But for every female who deserved a man's trust and respect, there was another like Abigail Jones. A schemer. A manipulator. A liar. She *was* lying. She had to be lying, because…

There was no *because.* She was as bad as he believed her to be. Worse even than Gillian, who had

had, at least at one time, some genuine feeling for him. Gillian's mistake had been in thinking Mac was so much in love with her he would never believe she could do what she had, in fact, done. Abbie's mistake was in coming to the Desert Rose, thinking she could manipulate him, and his family, into aiding and abetting her schemes.

It was just too bad she wasn't outside with him right now so he could tell her exactly what she could do with her malicious and misbegotten plans. Kicking at a bit of gravel, Mac headed for the darkened house, paying no attention to the sleepy sounds of a hot and humid night. A glimpse of movement, of something white where there should be only dark, caught his eye and he looked toward the lake and the section of dock that extended out into the water. Someone stood there and he told himself it might be his mother, out for a late-night walk around the ranch. Or maybe his aunt Vi, fretting about the fiftieth birthday that seemed to loom large and ponderously on her horizon. But even before the heels of his boots struck the redwood docking, he knew the figure bathed in moon glow was Abbie. Abbie, the schemer. Abbie, the liar. Abbie, with her hair curling loose and dusty gold about her shoulders. Abbie, with her face tilted to the night sky. Abbie, so beautiful his heart actually ached at the sight of her.

Which was crazy. He had fallen in love with an illusion. The mystery woman he had been dreaming of for five long months had never existed except in his imagination. And here was Abbie to prove it.

She turned at his approach, her hand grabbing the

dock railing, her expression tightening, her eyes narrowing, her shoulders stiffening as if she expected trouble. Well, she was right on that count. She could look like an angel all she wanted, with her hair streaked silver by the moonlight and the shape of her body outlined softly beneath the loose white shirt she wore. He *was* trouble. And she hadn't seen the half of it yet.

"Can't sleep?" he stopped, directly across from her, and leaned a hip against the railing. Fed by the boisterous Colorado River as it loped lazily through Texas, the lake lapped gently below the dock, lit by the light of a million stars and the shimmer of a moon reflected twice over in the dark water. "Conscience keeping you awake?"

"Heartburn," she said succinctly, turning in profile but clearly determined to stand her ground against him.

"Really? I've never been bothered by heartburn."

"Yet another example of how Mother Nature allows men to escape responsibility for their actions."

"Ah, now. I expected better from you than that old life-is-unfair-to-the-female line. A woman of your imaginative talents can surely do better than that worn-out excuse."

Her gaze settled on him, narrowed and cool. "Look, Prince Not Charming, I came out here to be alone with my thoughts, and while I know it's probably a lot to ask, I'd appreciate it if you left me the hell alone."

She was scrappy, he'd say that much for her. "Nicely put, but still just another lie."

"*Another* lie? You think I *want* you to stay out here and insult me?"

"I think if you'd wanted me to leave you the hell alone, you'd have stayed the hell away from me in the first place."

Her eyes narrowed to slits and he realized she wasn't wearing the black glasses, which was why, probably, he couldn't stop looking at her. That or the rather obvious fact that she didn't appear to be wearing anything but the oversize white shirt, which was certainly modest enough, although unsettling in its brevity. "I don't know how you ever managed to seduce me," she said tightly.

"Probably because it was the other way around. *You* seduced *me*."

"That's not the way I remember it."

"No, that's not the way you want *me* to remember it."

She sighed. "Okay, let me see if I've got your version of events down correctly. I planned the whole seduction. Bumped into you at the bar on purpose. Insisted on secrecy—no names, no phone numbers, no personal information. Had my wicked way with you all night, intentionally getting pregnant in the process. Slipped away the next morning, already plotting to run into you, by accident, five months later so I could make nefarious demands on your pristine name and fabulous fortune, which of course, I have researched to the last penny. Oh, yes, and then there's your oh-so-precious royal blue blood, which I traced all the way back to Lawrence of Arabia. Did I miss anything, Your Highness?"

He'd spent hours now going over just that scenario and, although it sounded ridiculous the way she said it, he thought there was as much evidence to support his theory as her claim that it was all sheer coincidence. Plus, he had the advantage of firsthand experience on just how duplicitous a woman could be and the lengths she would go to in order to get a wedding ring. "Only one small detail," he said, attempting to pierce her facade of innocent outrage with a hard stare. "I don't believe for a second I'm the father of that baby."

Her breathing grew instantly agitated at the implication and it seemed to take her several seconds to find the raspy sounds that passed for her voice. "All I can say is that if you're really a prince, the world is hard up for royalty."

"I don't believe my character is the one in question here."

"Well, you'll have to debate that with someone else." She turned and started to walk away. Barefoot. She was barefoot.

Mac pushed away from the dock rail and fell into step beside her, wondering if he should offer to carry her across the gravel driveway so she wouldn't hurt her bare feet. But she stopped short and faced him with a contemptuous glare. "What part of *leave me alone* do you not understand?"

Her chest rose and fell with each angry breath and he had a sudden, compelling impulse to rip off her concealing white shirt and bare her breasts so that he could see them full and ripe with her pregnancy. He found the idea of the changes in her body not just sexually titillating but exciting. Very exciting. And that realization unsettled him even further and made his voice scratchy and sharp. "You made a big mistake in coming to the Desert Rose. I don't know what you thought would happen here, but I can personally guarantee that you won't be happy with the outcome."

"That's already quite apparent," she said with an irritated sigh. "Because the *only* request I've made of you so far is to leave me alone."

He ought to do just that. He should take her lack of denial as validation and walk away from her right now. But this was his ranch, his home, his dock, and she'd contaminated them, along with the memories of the one night they'd spent together. He didn't know why the latter charge seemed the most offensive, but he'd be damned if he'd let it bother him. "I want you to leave tomorrow," he stated firmly, and hated the way his gut twisted in protest. "I know Jessica will try to persuade you to stay, but—"

"But it would be so much more comfortable for you if I go. You don't have to draw me a map. I understand I'm to make no claims on you for myself or for the baby." Her lips curved with a wry contempt. "But you know what? I can do that right here."

Mac frowned, waiting for fury at her defiant manner to sweep over him. "Do what?"

"Leave you alone, of course." Her chin was up, her eyes shining, as she gave an arrogant, decisive little toss of her head. "I'll stay here and work with Jessie as I planned and you'll stay out of my way and

I'll stay out of yours. Voilà, we both get what we want."

"You can't stay here," he said, not only not furious, but a little panicked. "That would be very unwise."

"Why? Are you going to run around behind my back, assuring everyone you're not the father of my baby?" She smiled, obviously of the opinion she had the upper hand. "That's only going to make them think it's a possibility."

"I have every right to defend myself."

"Against what? This?" She patted the slope of her belly. "Sorry, but you're a little late for that."

"You're not staying," he said, determined she would not best him in this argument. "Tomorrow, you'll tell Jessica that you've changed your mind and you must leave. Tomorrow, I'll drive you to the airport and pay for your ticket, if need be. But one way or another, tomorrow, you are leaving this ranch."

She turned her gaze back to the lake, looking both determined and satisfied with herself. "No, I don't think so."

"This isn't your decision."

Her eyes returned to him with the fire of her resolve. "Yes, Mac, it is. For five months now, I've rocked along, pretending this wasn't happening, putting off decisions, believing that if I ever met you again, you'd help me make the right choices for our baby. But I realize now, I am the responsible party here. And I will make the decisions without benefit of your advice. So, as far as I'm concerned, you and your arrogant, self-important opinions can take a flying leap into this lake and swim all the way to the Gulf of Mexico before I'll give half-a-second's consideration to what you want."

"My family will never permit you to claim any portion of the Desert Rose for your child."

"Your family will never know this child has every right to make such a claim unless you tell them."

"You expect me to believe you haven't already told them?"

"I've told no one. Except you. And believe me, if I could think of a way to take it back, you wouldn't know, either."

What could she hope to gain with this tack? Time? Opportunity? Support? "So you intend to hold me hostage here on my own property, while you wait for the right moment to drop your little bombshell?"

"I intend to stay as far away from you as you and the boundaries of this ranch will permit. But even if we step on each other every time we turn around, I am not going to be forced into leaving simply because my presence here makes you uncomfortable."

"You're making a mistake, Abigail Jones."

She stared silently into his eyes for a moment, then spun around and walked back to the end of the dock, reaching up with both hands to push the bulky weight of her hair off her nape. "Well, I made a mistake in not bringing a swimsuit, that's for sure."

Did she think she could simply announce her intention to make his life a living hell and then change the subject? Well, he could turn the tables as well as she. "What a pity," he said, unbuttoning his shirt. "A midnight swim would undoubtedly clear your head and enable you to think more clearly. It might even soothe your heartburn. But then again, probably not.''

''If you were a gentleman, you'd go away and the swimsuit would be a non-issue.''

His eyebrows went up. ''And leave you to swim alone? Now, that would be very *ungentlemanly.*''

''So it's okay to swim without a swimsuit as long as I don't do it alone?''

''Got it in one, Abigail Jones.'' He shrugged out of his shirt and tossed it over the rail, then his hands dropped to the buckle on his belt. ''The question is, are you going in with me or are you going to run away like a frightened little chicken?''

She turned around just as he unsnapped the top of his jeans. Her gaze flickered down the shadowy vee of hair on his chest to his abdomen, then rose in a guilty rush. ''Are you daring me to take my clothes off in full view of the house?''

''This is a working ranch. Anyone who's not asleep by this hour won't be worth a damn tomorrow. Besides, it would take a pair of high-powered binoculars to see this section of the dock from any of the ranch buildings in broad daylight, much less now.'' His gaze lingered on the exposed white skin of her inner arm as she continued to hold the weight of hair off her neck. Unbidden, he recalled the soft, sweet taste of her flesh in his mouth and knew the memory was as treacherous as her look of innocence, as tantalizing as the thought of her swimming naked beside him. He wanted to touch her, kiss her, bend her to his will. He wanted her to be who he'd believed she was, and that was impossible. Leaning against the dock rail, he balanced on one foot and pulled off first one boot, then the other. "So, little liar, are you brave enough to skinny-dip with me?"

"Brave, enough, yes. But not stupid. You'd probably try to drown me."

"Ah, good. You are afraid." He hooked his thumbs in the waistband of his jeans and she abruptly turned her back. "Although, I'd never resort to violence. As you're well aware, I have nothing to gain by harming you." He smiled at the stiff set of her shoulders and thought, with another nudge or two, she'd be eager to leave tomorrow. "So you see, Abbie, there's no reason for you to stand here in the heat and humidity, blaming me for depriving you of your swim. I already know you have no modesty."

Her chin came up as she whirled to face him, barely blinking at his state of undress. "You know nothing about me."

"I know you aren't going to risk letting me get a good look at a body heavy with the weight of another man's child. That could be detrimental to your plans."

If he'd been wearing any, his underwear would have gone down in flames. "You are the only man I've slept with in over a year," she said, her voice shaking with desperate anger. "And you are the father of this baby."

Mac considered her claim for a long moment, wondering, calculating the possibility, but he couldn't bring himself to believe her. He just couldn't. "Then, I guess you'll have to come up with another excuse to stay out of the water, won't you, little chick?'' He walked to the edge of the pier and stretched lazily, glancing at her over his shoulder. ''Oh, and don't bother pulling some juvenile stunt like stealing my clothes as you leave. I promise it would turn out to be far more embarrassing for you in the long run, if I have to walk back to the house in my birthday suit.'' Feeling that he'd successfully called her bluff, he made a clean, leisurely dive into the cool, cleansing water.

Abbie was reaching for the buttons of her shirt even before Mac completely disappeared beneath the surface. She'd show him she wasn't afraid of him or his stupid threats. She didn't care if he saw her body, rounding with the shape of the pregnancy. It was his fault she was in this shape, anyway. *Another man's child.* She should drown *him* for saying such a thing. For being such a jerk. How could she have been so stupid as to fantasize about him for the past five months, turning him into some kind of movie-idol hero in her mind, never imagining he'd reject her and the baby out of hand. It had never once occurred to her that he wouldn't believe her, that he'd accuse her of the blackest of lies and an attempt to trap him into marriage, as well.

Her fingers fumbled with the buttons. Going skinny-dipping to prove her point was only stooping to his level. It would do nothing more than make an awkward situation worse. But she couldn't just walk away, either. Retreat felt too much like surrender. She watched him, swimming in long, powerful strokes against the dark water, his muscular arms, legs, shoulders and buttocks visible in intermittent flashes of moonlit gold.

Okay, so if she wasn't going to strip naked and follow him in and she wasn't going to give him the satisfaction of her retreat, what other option did she have? Jumping in, fully clothed? Well, she was only wearing a white cotton shirt and a pair of maternity underpants, which would both be disgustingly revealing when dripping wet. If she'd had any idea she'd see anyone on this late night quest for a few moments of peace, she'd have put on something more suitable, although perhaps not as comfortable in this heat. On the other hand, if she'd known Mac was still out roaming the countryside like an alley cat, she'd never have ventured from her room in the first place, much less worried about what to wear.

Her gaze shifted to the clothes he'd flung carelessly across the dock railing. A paid of boots, socks, a belt, a pair of jeans, a denim…shirt. The first smile of the evening lifted her spirits. It wasn't the comeuppance she'd like to deliver him, by a long shot. On a scale of annoyance, it would barely rate a one and a half or a two, but it looked like her only option and therefore, it would have to do. In a matter of minutes, she was wrapped in his shirt, while hers hung, dry and waiting for her return, on the railing. As she rolled up the sleeves and turned down the collar, the scent of him surrounded her in a tide of memories that would be best forgotten. But for just a second…one little flashback of a moment…she remembered him as he'd been—as she'd thought he was—and wished things might have turned out differently. Then, arcing her hands high over her head, she dove straight and true into the water.

SHE SWAM LIKE A DADGUM DOLPHIN...and that bugged Mac even more than his sodden shirt. When he'd heard her hit the water with an efficient splash, he'd admired her spunk in choosing to take his dare rather than retreat. But when she managed to keep up with him—silently, but surely—regardless of the pace he kept, it didn't sit well.

It bothered him even more to realize she was not only a better swimmer than he was, but that she was enjoying this midnight exercise. She floated, she backstroked, she breaststroked, she butterflied. And when at last, she headed for the dock and climbed out of the water, he knew he'd outlasted her only by sheer obstinance. The fact that she'd used his shirt as a bathing suit might have rankled, if it hadn't clung to her with a dripping precision he was ashamed to find alluring. She turned her back to him and before he could shimmy into his jeans, she'd pulled off his shirt, wrung it out, wiped off some of the moisture that clung to her skin, and covered herself in the dry white oversize shirt she'd worn before. It clung to her breasts with a tantalizing dampness and cupped her hips in a teasing, patchy fashion that made his throat feel unaccountably dry and itchy.

"Here's your shirt," she said brightly, handing over the wet lump of denim. "Thanks."

"You're welcome. I'm always glad to lend an article of clothing to a damsel in distress." He'd meant to sound sarcastic, but somehow the words had come out gently, almost with a smile. "You want to borrow my boots? The ground between here and the house can be rough on bare feet."

She paused in the process of wringing lake water out of her long hair and looked at him as if trying to see the trap underlying such a gallant offer. "No, thanks. I'm tough."

"You're a very good swimmer."

"My brothers were competitive swimmers all through school and I spent a lot of time at swim meets when I was a kid. I wanted to swim competitively, too, but the family didn't think it was a suitable activity for a girl."

"And you let that stop you?"

Her lips curved a little as she wrung a few more droplets from her hair and straightened, twisting the wet strands into a thick loop across one shoulder. "Yes, I let that stop me."

"You've obviously developed a sense of independence since then."

Again she smiled in the same wistful, wry way. "Depends on who you ask."

This was nice, he thought. Pleasant, even. The immediate connection he'd made with this woman back in December returned to wisp around him like a vapor, elusive and enchanting, a witch's spell. Perhaps it was time to change tactics, try the sugar-rather-than-vinegar strategy, give her the rope she needed to hang herself. Never mind that he was fool enough to be enjoying the husky rhythms of her voice. Never mind that the night air carried a hint of her perfume. He had no earthly intention of referring to their previous encounter, but suddenly the words were in his mouth and on his tongue and out in the open. "Why did you leave without a word of goodbye?"

Her startled gaze hit him where it hurt and skittered away. "I…had someplace I had to be and it seemed best just…to go."

Mac finished pulling on his boots, knowing he was a fool to pursue this any further yet wanting her to understand what she might have had. "You have no idea how many times I've wished you had been there when I awoke."

The admission hung there, between them, a regret and a rebuke. "Hmm," she said finally. "A narrow escape for you then, wasn't it?"

The regret was suddenly pure and painfully his own. She turned and padded toward the end of the dock. Mac followed, watching the sway of her hips, the tint of moonlight on her dark, wet hair, and God help him, he wanted her. With every step, she contradicted him, tempted him, made him into the liar. And he hated that. He really did. At the end of the wooden planking, where the ground sloped in a sometimes rugged terrain up to the house, he caught up with her and scooped her into his arms.

"What the hell do you think you're doing?" she demanded, kicking lightly in protest.

"The ground's rough. You're barefoot." As if that explained it, which, of course, it didn't. He'd wanted to touch her, that was the gist of it. He'd wanted to know if the lust she evoked in him was susceptible to logic, if she, perhaps, still felt it, too. Apparently no to both points, he decided when she crossed her arms at her chest and stared stonily ahead. Holding her against his chest, he wanted to feel her arms around him, feel her melt into his embrace, kiss her long and hungrily to sate his own disreputable appetite. The moment he set her—bare feet unbruised by the rocky ground—on the tiled floor of the house, he fully expected to be rewarded with an outraged slap. The last thing he expected was what she did. She came up on tiptoe, the moist touch of her skin catching seductively against his, pulled his head down in a decidedly purposeful manner and kissed him full on the lips.

Electricity couldn't have zapped him more efficiently. Heat flared along his nerve endings and he wouldn't have been surprised if steam was coming off his hot body. He went weak in the knees with desire and knew he should not—*should not*—respond. This was a trick, another lie. But he gathered her abruptly into his arms and kissed her long and hard, as if she were the antidote as well as the poison. She returned pressure for pressure, desire for desire, as the kiss escalated and eventually eased. When he let her go, he was out of breath, confused and angry.

"You should be more careful, Prince," Abbie said in a tough, challenging whisper. "Any more rescues like that and you might find yourself in a very vulnerable position." And with that, she slipped out of his reach and ran lightly across the Mexican tiles, disappearing into the dark at the top of the stairs and leaving him to spend the rest of the night with a much harder question.

Chapter Four

Jessica hadn't exaggerated about the state of her office or the backlog of work. She'd rushed Abbie through breakfast and had her behind a desk almost before she had time to yawn. Jess spent less than fifteen minutes explaining the registration process, breeding, feeding and exercise schedules, boarding fees, stud fees, mare leasing, salaries, taxes, accounts payable, accounts receivable, and about a million other details that made up the bulk of business as usual on the Desert Rose. She dismissed Abbie's look of consternation with a laugh and the assurance that it would all become clear in the doing and that it was always okay to ask questions. Obviously, Abbie thought, ranching was a little more complicated than she'd expected. By noon, she'd lost count of the stacks of paper and manila files she'd sorted, logged, filed and straightened, but as Jess had predicted, she was beginning to get a feel for how the business worked, or at least, for how the office was supposed to run.

''I've decided,'' Jess said as they munched on the sandwiches and chips they'd wheedled from Jess's mother, Vi, in the bustling ranch house kitchen and carried back to the relative quiet of the office. It had been Abbie's idea to eat at their desks. She'd said she had a dozen questions, which was true enough, even if the motivating factor was to minimize any chance of crossing Mac's path.

"What? To fire me?" Abbie responded before crunching down on a chip.

"Nope. I've decided to keep you here forever, chained to that desk, if possible."

Abbie smiled. "There does seem to be enough backlogged paperwork in this one room to last a lifetime."

"Two lifetimes. Yours and mine. So, just forget any plans you have for the next forty years, because I have no intention of ever letting you leave."

"I have no plans, that's the problem. Well, except to give birth to this baby in a few months." She checked the firm, rounded bubble that had once been her waistline and raised her eyebrows as her glance returned to Jess. "Can you believe I've spent five whole months just getting used to the idea that I'm really going to have a baby?"

"It's a big idea to get a grip on." Jessie peeled away the crusts from one side of her sandwich and nibbled it, a strip at a time. "I'm just so glad you're here to help me, while you work out what you want to do."

"I want to go back five months and act responsibly." Abbie sighed, and frowned, then realized that was no longer true. She couldn't regret the life that was growing inside her, no matter how unintentionally it had begun. ''No, I guess I just wish I'd been more careful with whom I chose to be irresponsible and how I handled the situation afterward.''

''I take it he wasn't thrilled when you told him.''

''He didn't know.'' Abbie wondered if Mac would have taken the news any differently a few months ago and decided that he'd have reacted exactly the same, with perhaps the additional suggestion that she *take care of* the problem. ''I only just told him and, no, he's not thrilled.''

''You didn't tell him until recently?'' Jessie asked, clearly surprised.

Abbie realized she had wandered onto a dangerous line of conversation. ''The circumstances were sort of unusual.''

''He's married?''

Abbie shook her head and pinched off a bite of sandwich, which she chewed rhythmically as she let the question settle. ''No, he's not married,'' she said eventually, determined to move on to other topics. ''Just a jerk.''

''I didn't even know you were dating anyone. I'd hoped to introduce you to one of my cousins at graduation, but I guess it wasn't meant to be.''

Abbie avoided choking by asking, ''Which cousin?''

Jess shrugged and reached for the chip bag. ''At the time, I'd have settled for any one of the three falling head over heels for you, but Mac was my first choice. That's funny, huh? Especially since the two of you didn't hit it off too well the first time you did meet.''

Actually, she and Mac had hit it off extremely well the first time they met, which was why she was in her current predicament.

"Oh, well," Jessie continued, cheerfully sorting through the handful of corn chips in her palm. "If I can't finagle you into a love match with Mac, my only available cousin, I'll just have to pay you so well you can't afford to work anywhere else." She crunched the selected chip. "Either that, or I'll fix you up with Stanley. He's a trainer who comes in three times a week to give lessons and work with some of the boarders. He's old enough to be your father, but I think you might like him." She grinned and Abbie found herself grinning back.

"Just what I need," she said. "Another father figure. As if I didn't already have a father *and* four big brothers who want to run my life."

"I'm only kidding about Stanley." Jessie wiped her hands on a paper towel, wadded it up and tossed it into the trash. "He's a great guy, but I've been saving him as my backup in case I never happen across the right frog to kiss and turn into my very own handsome prince."

"There seems to be a surplus of princes on the Desert Rose," Abbie said. "Don't they have any prince friends?"

Jessie laughed. "And here I was, hoping you might introduce me to one of your brothers. I mean, if I can't interest you in my cousin, the only way for us to become related is if I hook up with one of the Joneses, right?"

Abbie had never thought about fixing up her friend

with her brother. Any one of them. She adored them all, of course, but they were so overbearing. ''I can arrange for you to meet them and take your pick,'' she offered with a smile. ''But I warn you, you'll be happier in the long run if we just stay good friends.'' She paused for a second, wanting again to express her gratitude for Jessie's friendship. ''I'm going to pay you back for all this, Jess, I promise. I don't know what I would have done if you hadn't been so generous and offered me this temporary—''

''Don't mention it,'' Jessie said, her eyes of different colors smiling with equal sincerity. ''You are doing me the biggest favor ever and you've repaid me a dozen times over just this morning. I was really afraid when you got here yesterday that you weren't going to stay.''

''It was a stressful day and I'm still wondering if I shouldn't have just gone on home and faced the music.''

''You did the right thing, coming here, Abbie. And I'm not saying that just because I need the help. You owe yourself and your baby some time to decide what to do. You've waited this long to deal with your family. Another few weeks won't make any difference. And it's not as if you owe them an explanation. You're pregnant, not an escapee from the penitentiary.''

''Oh, I don't know. If I was on the lam, my brothers could spend their considerable energy hiding me from the authorities. But with a baby, they'll have a whole new life to interfere in.''

''Okay, so maybe I'm too independent to pair up

with one of your brothers. On the other hand, maybe it's just your time to stand up to them. I've heard that having a baby brings out a fiercely protective streak in a woman.''

''Maybe,'' Abbie agreed. ''But I'm still in the cowardly stage. I'm dreading the moment they find out about the baby, because I know my brothers, and they won't be thinking in terms of how much fun it could be to be an uncle. They'll be thinking in terms of murdering the man who dared to have sex with their sister.''

''Sounds like just what the jerk deserves. I say, turn them loose.'' Jessica dusted sandwich crumbs off her desk blotter and then pulled an inch-high stack of manila folders onto the cleared spot. ''Guess it's just as well, though, that he's out of reach. They might decide you ought to marry the guy and then where would you be? Shotgun wedding, that's where.''

Abbie hadn't thought about that possibility. Not that anyone could force her to marry Mac, the princely jerk. Not even her four very persuasive, very determined brothers. ''Great,'' she said. ''One more thing for me to worry about.''

Jessie laughed. ''I was only kidding, goose. Even if the Jones men showed up this very minute, they'd have a heck of a time insisting you marry an invisible man, now wouldn't they? Forget your troubles for today, Abbie. I mean it. You're safe at the ranch. Believe me, nobody here is going to bother you.''

Abbie tossed aside her paper towel, including most of her sandwich. Truth was, somebody at this ranch was already bothering her. Here, where she should have been free to ponder the future and make her decisions with confidence, she was faced with muddled emotions and uncertainties. Here, she'd run head-on into a problem greater than the authoritarian but loving mantle of her family's concern. Here, she had to face Mac and the unsettling knowledge that, after last night's ill-conceived kiss, she was still stupidly but undeniably attracted to him.

SLIPPING QUIETLY into the viewing area of the indoor arena, Mac settled onto a riser and leaned forward, resting his arms on the metal rail. Olivia Smith was alone in the ring with a sleek black mare and her dusky colt, who at four months of age was already displaying the superb physical attributes and proud temperament of his sire, Jabbar, the Desert Rose foundation stallion. The colt, Khalid, was the result of a happy accident, when Jabbar—proving to be amazingly virile for an old fella—wound up in the same pasture with Alex's recently purchased show mare, Khalahari. It had been touch-and-go when the mare went into labor, but Dr. Hannah Clark, who had since become Alex's bride, had proved herself a hell of a good vet, and saved both mom and foal.

Khalid had the bloodlines and aptitude of a champion, but at the moment, he was mainly interested in the treats Livy kept in her pockets and doled out as rewards each time he made a little progress. Mac believed in starting a foal in training within a few days of birth and Khalid had been no exception, but today he seemed to be having trouble concentrating. Livy, however, wasn't putting up with any horseplay and

Mac smiled as the feisty colt and equally feisty trainer squared off in a battle of wills over who would be boss.

Watching the two go at it, Mac knew he'd done the right thing by letting Olivia train Jabbar's last offspring. He'd wanted to do it himself, had wrestled with his ego for weeks before the birth, but in the end he decided Livy had more energy and a purer concentration. It wasn't that he lacked confidence in his own abilities. On the contrary, he considered himself the best trainer of Arabians in the country. His success was witnessed by the consistent wins of the animals he trained and the number of owners vying for the occasional vacant spots in his training schedule. Mac had known even as a kid that he possessed an unusual and intuitive knowledge of what a horse was capable of doing and the best way to inspire that potential into reality. But, young as she was—a mere twenty-three—Olivia had a gift that rivaled his already. She'd developed an almost mystical bond with the young Khalid and he could see that one day, when she'd matured and honed her talents, her skill would surpass his. He felt twinges of competition about that and was, by turns, motivated by her ability and then eager to best her in any way he could.

But he was nobody's fool and he intended to do whatever it took—even if it meant an occasional fight with his own ego—to keep her working for the Desert Rose. More than any other factor, her value to the ranch had prompted him to let her work with Khalid. "I think he's going to be in good shape for his class at the show next week," he said.

"He'll win," Livy announced confidently, her orphaned but resilient spirit alive and well in her petite, slim frame.

Mac wasn't a dreamer like Livy, choosing to temper his wishes with a healthy both-boots-on-the-ground pragmatism. He admired her speak-the-words-and-claim-the-goal optimism, even if he didn't believe life was that simple. And to back up that theory, all he had to do was look out at the lake, remember Abbie standing on the dock last night in his drenched denim shirt, and he had all the evidence he needed.

"I'm driving in to Austin to meet with Dale," he said referring to another trainer who was negotiating fiercely to breed a mare from his stables to the retired Jabbar. "Be back late, so I'd appreciate it if you'd exercise the chestnut gelding for me this afternoon."

"Sure," Livy said, snapping the lead to get Khalid's attention and then offering him soft words of praise and a tangible reward when he responded with a show-quality arching of his supple neck. "But I thought you met with Dale yesterday."

He had, before he'd gone to the airport to meet Abbie, but no one needed to know he wasn't meeting the trainer again today. Once in a while, a man had to get away from it all and have some space to think. In the twenty-four hours since Abbie's arrival, he'd been doing a lot of thinking, and expended a considerable amount of energy on keeping away from her. A strategy that seemed to be working better today than it had last night. His lips burned with the memory of her full, wet kiss and his body hardened at the image of her, dripping and desirable. He shoved the memory into oblivion, where it surely belonged, along with all the gullible fantasies he'd concocted about her during the past five months. "You know what a pest Dale can be," he said to Olivia. "He won't stop pestering me until he gets a colt from Jabbar, even though I keep telling him Khalid was just an accident."

"Well, tell him no and be done with it. You never have any trouble saying no around here." Livy turned to grin at him and Khalid seized the opportunity to kick the air with his back legs and momentarily gain the upper hand.

"How many times do I have to remind you, Livy? You can't take your eyes off him for a second. This kid has his own agenda."

Livy's chin went up and her attention returned, full-strength, to the colt. Straight away, she let him know his lack of respect was unacceptable and Mac grinned to himself, pleased with the progress both youngsters were making. Feeling the touch of a gaze, he looked over his shoulder and saw his mother, Rose, standing just inside the arena. She was looking at him, her lovely face cast in shadows. He'd seen that expression often since she'd arrived at the Desert Rose, a few months ago. It was as if she couldn't choose between the happiness of finally being with her sons or sorrow for the years she'd been kept away from them. For him, it was no contest. After believing his mother dead for much of his life, it was a simple, sweet delight to glance up and see her now. He smiled and scooted over on the bench, silently inviting her to join him, which she did.

''Khalid is very like his sire, I think,'' she said softly. ''He reminds me of Jabbar at that age, in much the same way you remind me of your father.''

''Headstrong, you mean?''

She smiled and touched his hair, like a soft and thankful prayer. ''Proud,'' she replied. ''Strong. Determined. Certain that your way is the right way. Ibrahim chose your name rightly. Makin. It means strong, firm, and it suits you.''

Mac didn't believe for a second that any strength or resolve he'd inherited came entirely from his father. Rose had proved the depths of her courage and determination before Mac was even old enough to know the meaning of the words. Countless times, he'd heard the story of how his mother, with help from her sister-in-law, Layla, had smuggled him and his two brothers along with Jabbar, who'd been but a colt then, himself, out of Sorajhee. He knew by rote the events leading up to the unrest and feared revolution that had precipitated their flight from the country of his birth. But he didn't remember any of it. Not even a shadowy memory of his father, King Ibrahim, could be found. In his heart, he was a Texan, his aunt Vi and uncle Randy were the only parents he'd known, and this ranch, this rugged hill country was the only place he could ever imagine calling home. Maybe, in the future, he'd visit Sorajhee and Balahar from time to time, as Cade and Serena meant to do, but he knew it would never claim more than a corner of his life and that his journeys to that land of sun and sand would never be more than a pilgrimage he owed to the Sorajhee king who had been his father.

"You're looking particularly pretty today." He paid his mother the compliment with sincerity and a soft smile and was surprised when her cheeks flushed a delicate pink. She was still a beautiful woman with a grace honed by tragedy, and in the brief time he'd actually known her, she had begun to bloom like a true rose after a long, frozen winter. "The dry heat of Texas obviously agrees with you."

"I love the heat," she said. "I missed the warmth during all those years in France. It always seemed so cold there."

"A sanitarium isn't exactly what anyone would consider a warm place to call home."

Her lips curved in acknowledgment. "It was not a terrible place. But that is all behind us now. I am with you and Alex and Cade again. Family is all that matters."

Mac privately thought the stream of letters she'd received lately—all of them bearing the royal seal of King Zakariyya Al Farid of Balahar—might have a little something to do with her new blush of contentment. Cade and Serena believed the communication between Serena's father and Rose was more than an exchange of congratulations on the love match between their children. Mac had been skeptical when Cade first suggested the idea, but he was beginning to think there was something to it, after all. "Has the mail come today?" he asked, and watched for the return of the tell-tale blush.

It came in a soft wave of pink across her cheeks,

but her blue eyes met his with clear purpose. ''Yes, as a matter of fact, it has. You should probably go to the office right now and see if whatever you are expecting is there.''

''I'm not *expecting* anything,'' he answered, his voice edgy with a sudden influx of tension. ''And I certainly have no business in the office.''

''Hmm,'' Rose said, her gaze turning to Olivia and Khalid, as if her second son's crisp denial was of no consequence. ''Jessica's friend, Abbie, is quite lovely. I thought you might have noticed.''

''She's pregnant,'' he said, as if she might have missed the obvious.

Rose laughed softly. ''Ah, you are afraid of her condition. Many men would be. Now I understand why you wish to avoid her.''

Mac blinked, beginning to think his mother had insights he'd just as soon she didn't have. ''I'm not afraid of her,'' he stated confidently. ''Her condition has nothing at all to do with me and she hasn't even been here twenty-four hours yet. How can anyone think I'm avoiding her?''

Rose's brows arched in gentle reproach. ''It was a simple comment, Makin. I only spent a brief time in conversation with Abbie, but she seems a lovely girl and someone with whom you have common interests. I did not intend to upset you.''

''I'm not upset,'' he lied, although it was plenty obvious he was. Abbie was already ruining his life, going behind his back and making friends with his mother. That, in itself, was a low-down, rotten thing to do. ''And I don't know how you could think I'd have anything at all in common with her.''

''Jessica has believed for some time that you and her friend would like each other, but now she believes you said something to offend Abbie.''

Great. Abbie had managed to get Jess on her side and had planted the idea that he'd somehow offended her. It spoke to her devious nature that in such a short amount of time, she'd already instigated speculation about him between his cousin and his mother. Probably Aunt Vi had been included in the discussion, as well. She and Rose seemed to be spending a lot of time together lately and enjoying their long-delayed friendship. But if his absence from dinner last night, breakfast and lunch today, along with skipping his normal trip into the office to harass Jess this morning, was being commented upon and attributed to Abbie's presence, he would only give the idea credence by denying it. ''I can't really remember what I said, but I certainly don't recall it being anything that could possibly have been offensive to her, unless her condition just makes her hypersensitive.''

Rose looked at him closely, then turned to watch Olivia and Khalid again. ''He has a stubborn streak, too,'' she said. ''Just like his father.''

Mac pushed up from the riser, feeling as if he had to get moving in any direction that Abbie—and the subject of Abbie—wasn't. ''I have an appointment this afternoon in Austin,'' he said. ''Lest anyone think I'm avoiding her…or him.''

Rose's smile seemed suddenly full of secrets. ''Be safe, my son.''

"Always," he replied, and tried to act as if he hadn't a worry in the world as he strode away.

ROSE REMAINED in the viewing area after Livy gave Jabbar's colt a final reward and led him, along with Kalahari, into the attached barn. Inhaling the horsey smell of the arena and the woodsy scent of the shavings, she experienced a pang of homesickness for Sorajhee, where she had known such great happiness. She knew full well that she was a fortunate woman to have loved Ibrahim, even if his murder had cut short so many of her dreams. But she had his sons—Alim, Makin, Kadar—finally, wondrously returned to her, and with today's mail, the possibility that the baby that had been taken from her at birth was alive and too much like Ibrahim to be anyone else's son. Sharif. The adopted son of her husband's ally. It had stunned her to see his face among those in the pictures of the wedding of Kadar and Serena in Balahar. At first, she'd believed it was an hallucination, a throwback to the vivid dreams she'd experienced in the sanitarium. But then, slowly, as she listened to Serena talk about her father, King Zak of Balahar, and her brother, the crown prince, Rose had begun to see that the son she'd delivered during those first dark months of her confinement could be miraculously restored to her. She'd written King Zak already, stating her belief that Sharif was her birth son. It was a precious secret she held close to her heart. There would be time enough to share it when the truth was finally discovered. She would wait for Zak's answer before she raised any hopes other than her own.

"Hi," Livy said shyly, returning from the barn sans colt and mare. "I'm finished inside for today, but I think Stanley Fox is working with a couple of horses in the outdoor ring, if you want to watch."

Rose smiled, liking this pixie of a woman-child, with her violet eyes and wild, wispy brown hair. "Thank you, but I am content where I am. You have an extraordinary gift."

"With the horses, you mean?" Livy looked down, brought her gaze up again. "I guess, maybe. Mac says I might grow into a good trainer."

"My brother has told me that Makin had an almost mystical bond with the horses even at a very young age. He recognizes that gift in you, as well, or he would never have given over the training of Jabbar's last colt to you."

Livy's face flushed with pleasure and she came nearer, leaning against the rail that separated the arena from the viewing risers. "I heard about the way you smuggled Jabbar and your sons out of the country where they were born. That must have been pretty scary, even for a queen."

Rose heard the awed emphasis on the title and smiled into Olivia's brightly curious eyes. "It was such a long time ago," she said. "And so much has happened since, I honestly cannot remember being afraid, although I'm sure I was."

"It's like you lived a real fairy tale, marrying a prince from another country, becoming queen when he was crowned king, and then having to escape when he was killed." A frown crossed Livy's face and she caught her lower lip between her teeth. "I'm sorry, that was a tactless thing to say. I just get sort of caught up in stories about Arabian Nights and Arabian princes who ride out of the desert and sweep unsuspecting princesses away to the Casbah." She blushed furiously. "Comes from the reading material I found at the orphanage, I guess. Anyway, it's probably painful for you to remember and I shouldn't have brought it up. I'm just..." Her explanation trailed into an embarrassed silence.

"You're just curious," Rose said, believing she could understand some of the fantasies a young orphan might nurture within the walls of her loneliness. "I had something of a fantasy about a desert prince when I was young, too, and you know what?" She was rewarded when Livy's eyes reclaimed their inquisitive sparkle. "It came true. Well, except for him riding out on a white stallion and sweeping me away."

"He drove a car, huh?" Livy wanted to know.

"No, the stallion was black. Jabbar's sire, in fact. A beautiful animal, but I had eyes only for the man who rode him." The memory of Ibrahim's courtship flooded her with sweet pleasure, and she savored it for a moment before focusing again on the young woman before her. "The part of the fairy tale that is absolutely true, though, Livy, is the part where the princess falls deeply in love with the prince. I loved my prince and it wouldn't have mattered to me if he'd chosen to be a tour guide instead of a king. I loved him for who he was, with or without his royal titles. Keep that in mind, when you are imagining your own happy ending."

"Oh, I don't think about that anymore." But Livy's answer was too rushed, too emphatic and besides, Rose recognized the blush. There was a bit of a princess in every woman, she supposed, and maybe the glimmer of a prince in every man. "I just wondered, you know, what it was like to be a real queen."

"Until the last couple of months in Sorajhee, it was the happiest time of my life. But now...well, now, I'm very happy to be living here on the Desert Rose with my family."

"It seems like you've always lived here. I guess you always have, in spirit, anyway. I mean, even the ranch is named for you."

It was a sweet thing to say and Rose stood with a smile. "Thank you, Olivia," she said. "If I had had a daughter, I like to think she might have been something like you."

Livy didn't reply, but as Rose walked out of the arena, she thought she heard a soft, jaunty, tuneful whistling of "Some Day My Prince Will Come."

ABBIE WALKED THROUGH THE BARN casting glances into each and every box stall she passed, whether it was occupied or not. For their part, the horses in the stalls observed her presence with varying degrees of interest. "Hello," she whispered to one who twitched her perky ears in response. "Hello there," she said to another, who ignored her completely, although his neighbor in the next box nickered in soft reply. Horses, Abbie was discovering, were as individual as the humans who loved them. In the two days she'd been at the ranch, she'd already learned more than she'd ever realized there was to know about ranches and the breeding, training and showing of Arabian horses. She'd done a damn good job of staying out of Mac's way, too, possibly because he'd virtually vanished since her arrival. Well, except for that little interlude by the lake. But since then, she hadn't even caught sight of his cowboy hat in the distance.

Which was fine with her. The less she had to see of him, the better. Unfortunately, Jessie was quick at jumping to conclusions based on little or no evidence and kept saying things to indicate she thought Mac's behavior odd in the extreme and connected, somehow, to Abbie's arrival. If Abbie had been a little less distracted herself, she'd have kept her mouth shut instead of thoughtlessly answering Jess's questions. But the queries had been so subtle, so innocuous on the surface, it hadn't occurred to Abbie to be on her guard. Then suddenly, she realized she'd expressed her belief that the baby would have dark eyes, dark hair, skin that turned a rich golden-brown in the sun, and since she possessed none of those traits, she'd essentially described the basic appearance of her baby's father. Maybe that in itself wouldn't have been so incriminating until Jess asked casually about the due date and counted quickly—and accurately—back to the end of December and the graduation party. Panicking just a bit, Abbie confessed that she'd met a mystery man that night, but she hadn't even found out his name as she'd never expected to see him again.

The truth circled back around on her and in practically no time, Jess was mentioning Abbie's remark that she had *recently* told the father about her pregnancy. From there, it was just a hop, skip and a jump to the question about when, exactly, and where she'd run into this mysterious stranger again and how embarrassing that must have been and what on earth had he said and wasn't Abbie going to insist he, at least, pay child support? After all, the baby was as much his responsibility as Abbie's, no matter if he wanted to admit it or not. Then Abbie was explaining that he didn't even believe the baby was his, a tactic that seemed to halt the questions in midstream. Jess seemed preoccupied after that, but even after going over and over the conversation in her head, Abbie didn't believe anything she'd said pointed directly to Mac as the father. Still she'd have to be more careful from now on. More guarded in what she said. More conscious of where a perfectly innocent question could lead.

Glancing at her watch, Abbie felt the tension knot in her stomach as she lifted the cell phone from her pocket and, with a deep inhale, punched in the auto dial for home. Probably the barn wasn't the best place to make the call, but reception in her bedroom was sketchy and she didn't want one or all of her brothers deciding she needed a new cell phone with a broader range of service. That would mean, of course, that they'd have to deliver it en masse and in person so they could give her instructions on how to work the silly thing. "Hi, there," she said brightly when Brad answered on the first ring. "I'm checking in, as directed and—I'll have you note—a few minutes early."

He laughed, as if the last thing he'd ever do was worry if his kid sister failed to call at a certain time, certain day, certain exact moment. "How's it going, kiddo? You tired of being a camp counselor, yet?"

"Hardly. I'm having a great summer!" It was an effort, but she infused her voice with a camper's enthusiasm. "The kids are great, the camp is great, I'm great. Couldn't be better."

"Well, maybe you should give it a couple more days," he said, his tone indulgent in humoring her. "You haven't even been there a week. I've got to tell you, Abs, Mom isn't happy that you couldn't find two minutes to get home for a visit before you hightailed it out of Miss Amelia's Academy and headed for the Poconos."

"You're the one who wasn't happy about that." She called his bluff. "Mom and I talked and she understood the timing just wasn't right. I'd have been exhausted from the traveling instead of having those couple of days to get my bearings here."

"Well, we expect to see you soon. Forget this nonsense about going the whole summer without seeing your family. Otherwise, we may just have to show up there for Parents' Day."

Panic. Abbie forced a gay laugh. "Ha-ha. You won't show up that day, for sure. I wouldn't have five seconds to spend with you. It'll be utter chaos here."

"Okay, then. Name another weekend. Or better yet, save us a fortune in plane fares and get yourself a weekend pass."

"Good idea," she lied, then rushed on to ask, "Who else is there? Jaz? Ty? Mom, Dad?"

"Every last one of us," he said. "Just waiting for the chance to hear your voice and make sure you're okay. Who do you want to talk to next? Quinn?"

Finding a bale of hay, Abbie sank onto it, giving her shaky legs a break and herself a good view of the open doorway, in case any of the Desert Rose residents walked by and came close enough to overhear. "Let me say hi to Dad first," she requested, and then spent the next thirty minutes trying to say as little as possible and get off the line without arousing even a single suspicion that practically everything she did say was an outright and outrageous lie.

JESSICA DISCREETLY EYED her cousins as they argued good-naturedly over whether Mac had cheated the last time the two of them had drawn straws to settle a disagreement. It was the way they'd almost always settled their disputes, at least the ones that could be resolved with a straw broken into two unequal parts. Jessie couldn't imagine herself in such a contest with anyone. She'd prefer a battle of wills any day. But it worked for the twins. This last time, it had worked out especially well, bringing Cade and Serena together...first in a marriage of convenience and then in a ceremony that celebrated their true love match.

At the moment, Cade was laughing at Mac's assertions that he always got cheated by his younger—by twenty-three minutes—brother. Jessie had never seen the younger twin so happy or the older one less so. Oh, Mac was putting a good face on it—playfully teasing his sister-in-law about how if only Mac had drawn the shorter straw, Serena wouldn't have had to marry the runt of the litter. It was nonsense, of course, said playfully and meant only to complement the newlyweds' obvious bliss. Serena was fathoms deep in love with her Prince Charming, as was he with her, and Mac was supremely content to be the only remaining bachelor sheikh on the Desert Rose.

Or was he? Jessica had a glimmering of an idea—a crazy and persistent idea—that somehow, some way Mac and Abbie had met somewhere before he'd picked her up at the airport, had—and this was the crazy part—actually met the night of the big graduation party. Which would make Mac not only Abbie's mystery man, but the father of her baby. Jessie knew that had to be all but impossible, and yet the idea persisted, growing more and more appealing as the answer to why Mac was avoiding Abbie and Abbie was avoiding Mac and why, when they did happen to be in the same room, like now, neither of them came within right angles of looking at the other. It gave some justification for Abbie's pale and edgy arrival at the ranch and a reason for Mac to have been madder than a jackrabbit with a crooked ear when he dropped her off. It went a long way toward explaining why Mac had been so inquisitive about Jessie's school friends in the months since her graduation.

Jessie knew she was daydreaming, trying to put together a theory that was more than likely based on a faulty equation, but it had tumbled into her mind and wouldn't be dismissed. Something was wrong about Abbie sitting on one side of the family room, talking quietly with Hannah, while Mac sat on the other side, pitching his voice a little too loudly, a tad too merrily to go unnoticed.

He was making an effort to prove his total indifference to Abigail Jones, and convincing Jessie, if no one else, that he was so aware of Abbie he could hardly think straight. It would have been funny if it wasn't so serious. Abbie was pregnant and, although it was hard to believe, the more she thought about it, the more Jessica believed the baby belonged to Mac.

''I didn't cheat.'' Mac laughed, his glance never shifting anywhere near Abbie. ''You held the straws. All I did was pick one. How can it be my fault that I got the longer straw?''

''All I'm saying,'' Cade said, his voice and laughter a perfect duplicate of Mac's, ''is that it seems odd you lose so often. That's all.''

''Well, look at it this way,'' Mac replied. ''You may have drawn the short straw this last time, but it turned out to be the luckiest thing that ever happened to you, now, didn't it?''

Cade, so much like Mac it was scary, turned to smile at the green-eyed, auburn-haired Serena, who smiled back, leaned forward and kissed him lightly on the lips. ''I *am* the luckiest Texas sheikh there ever was,'' Cade said.

''And a most fortunate Sorajhee sheikh, who is son-in-law to the king of Balahar,'' Serena added, teasing. ''Perhaps you should insist that Mac begin now to call you Prince Kadar.''

''Not in this lifetime,'' Mac replied with a grin. ''The day I have to call this guy by some highfalutin title, I'm packin' my cowboy boots and heading for the high country.''

Over in her corner of the room, Abbie laughed softly in her conversation with Hannah, Rose and Vi. Jessie kept her gaze on Mac and watched his shoulders stiffen with tension at the sound. Her theory had some holes, to be sure, but she hadn't seen anything yet that discredited it. In fact, the longer she thought about it, the more plausible it seemed. Mac and Abbie had met by accident rather than design at the graduation party. They'd spent the night together and, for whatever reason, agreed to go their separate ways the following morning. Mac was the father of Abbie's baby. It was the only reason the two of them could be acting as if they were oblivious to the other, when clearly neither of them was oblivious at all.

Still she couldn't just blurt out that she'd figured out the reason for their silent hostility. She wasn't certain she was right, only almost certain. So if she couldn't just ask if she'd gotten the right answer, she'd do her best to throw them together over the next few days and see what kind of fireworks she set off. Starting tomorrow morning, avoiding each other was going to become an exercise in frustration for both her cousin and her friend. It made Jessie grin like a kid with a snow cone just thinking about it.

Chapter Five

Amazing, Abbie thought. A week ago she'd barely known one end of a horse from the other and today she was on her way to a horse show. As an exhibitor, no less. Well, in truth, she was just a warm body, another pair of hands, someone to fetch coffee or hamburgers for the Desert Rose staff, make phone calls, mend costumes or simply be willing to do whatever needed doing. No-brainer stuff, Jessica had termed it, claiming she'd have loved to go herself, if only she could get away from the office, if only Nick Grayson—the son and heir of her father's business partner—wasn't the bane of her existence and hadn't demanded she deliver immediately—if not *sooner!*—a detailed report only she could produce. It wasn't fair, of course, Jess had admitted, but would Abbie please, *please* consider going in her place?

After a gentle probing of who exactly attended these shows—this one in particular—and figuring out Mac wasn't on the list, Abbie agreed that she would. She did, in fact, want to go. It sounded fun and exciting, a chance to see the stars of the Desert Rose show their stuff, and an opportunity to see what

Mac's vocation was really about. True, she hadn't known what she was letting herself in for, didn't know from that point on in the week, Jessie would insist she spend more time in the barn than in the office, learning the basic tenets of horse care, if nothing else. Abbie had learned a great deal, as it happened, almost all of it from Mac, who was so consistently present she felt she couldn't open her eyes without running into his disapproving gaze.

Abbie had been slower on the uptake than perhaps Sherlock Holmes would have been, but it didn't take her long to deduce that Jessica's agenda included more than a report to the Coleman-Grayson corporate offices in Dallas. The first time Olivia was called away unexpectedly during the rookie training sessions and replaced by an overtly disgruntled Mac could have been accidental, but the second time it happened, Abbie suspected there was some sort of matchmaking afoot. Jessie, thinking with her generous heart, had decided to see if she couldn't spark a romance between her cousin and her friend. It was about five months too late for romance, but Abbie found the misguided gesture endearing all the same. If the notion of matchmaking had occurred to Mac, he was clearly against the idea.

"What do you think you're trying to prove?" he'd asked curtly when she refused to slink quietly away the second time he walked in to summon Livy to the phone and caught Abbie measuring out grains for feeding. "I thought you agreed to stay out of my barn."

Abbie didn't think he deserved an explanation, even if she'd been inclined to offer one. "Jess sent me to learn the basics. She seems to think the barn and the activities in it are an important part of the business, which I believe, belongs to the Coleman-Grayson Corporation, of which you are merely one of the shareholders.''

''Major shareholders,'' he corrected.

''Yes, well, thanks very much for your kind offer to instruct me, but I'll just wait for Livy to come back.''

''Livy has to get ready for this week's horse show. She doesn't have time to baby-sit a greenhorn, like you.'' His sigh was a masterpiece of frustration. ''What is it you want to know?''

''Everything,'' Abbie had replied with a tight, crisp smile, mentally tallying up a point for her side.

And so, the week had begun. Beneath a glower befitting royalty, Mac had taught her a little about a lot. Not by so much as a glance did he say anything personal. He maintained a significant distance between them at all times and kept the conversation on a need-to-know basis. If she asked a question, he answered. If he was offering information, he did it in as few words as would suffice and all with an exaggerated show of indifference. Abbie tried to follow his instructions to the letter in the interest of learning and—although she hated to admit it—in the hope of winning at least one glimmer of approval.

The approval never came, but she took some small satisfaction in the fact that whenever Livy offered to take over the lessons, he growled that she had more important things to do and curtly sent her off to do them. He said nothing else about the upcoming horse show to Abbie and, since she was pretty certain he would try to prevent her from going if he knew, she didn't mention it, either. It wasn't, she decided, any of his business.

But suddenly, now that she was sitting beside him on the bench seat in the cab of his wicked black truck, and they were already en route to Dallas and the Arabian Horse Show, she wished she'd told him straight out that she was going. He was simmering over there behind the steering wheel, his dark eyes as steely cold with anger as she'd ever seen them. And she'd seen them angry plenty of times in the week she'd been at the Desert Rose. It was probably pointless to tell him that Jessie was behind this enforced togetherness, that it was his cousin who'd engineered the whole scheme, right down to the small delay that resulted in Abbie barely making it out of the office before the convoy left. She didn't know how Jess had managed it, but, somehow, by the time the trucks pulled away from the Desert Rose ranch, every seat was taken, save one. The one beside Mac.

"I want you to know," she said, because she couldn't let the blistering accusation in his silence stand, "this was not my idea."

"It sure as hell wasn't mine." He checked the trailer in the rearview mirror and increased his speed by a very few miles an hour. Slow and steady seemed to be the watchword as the four trucks and trailers formed a convoy on Highway 73 and headed toward the junction with Interstate 35 just east of Austin. "And don't bother trying to convince me it was Jess's idea, either."

"She asked me to take her place." Abbie adjusted the seat belt strap to a more comfortable and safer position beneath the baby's weight. "You must know I wouldn't have agreed to go if I'd known you were going."

"You knew I'd be going."

She tensed at the accusation. "Jessie said you weren't. She told me if you attended at all, you'd drive down late and leave early. She said most of the time, you don't bother going to shows because you feel your job is done once the horse is trained and ready to show."

"Hogwash," he said succinctly. "I haven't missed the Dallas show since I turned nine and won my first championship ribbon. As for the rest, I probably wind up attending about twenty shows a year, sometimes more. Most often, I go early and stay late. The Desert Rose is famous all over the world for our stock, but it's these shows that keep our name out there, give our horses and our people the recognition they deserve and work so hard to earn. Training and showing Arabians is my business and I'm damn good at it. I wouldn't willingly miss an important show and Jessie knows it." He cast a cynical and gloomy gaze at her. "My cousin may have a lot to answer for this week, but I don't believe this particular miscalculation is on the list."

Abbie's face flushed with annoyance. "So in addition to being a pathological liar, I'm guilty of…what? Scheming to go to the horse show? Stealing trade secrets to pass on to your competition?"

The corner of his mouth pulled into a wry smile. "If you think I shared any secrets with you this week, you didn't learn much about horses, or me. I barely introduced you to the most basic, beginner kind of stuff, nothing even close to insider information."

"Then I must be plotting some other nefarious way to ruin your life." She flounced as best she could, considering the restraint of the seat belt and her pregnancy. "Because, of course, I wouldn't want to waste my time learning about a subject simply because it interests me."

"I'll confess I was surprised you stuck with it." His gaze settled on her, sending a prickling, titillating awareness skittering across her nape. "I'm even a little flattered you went to so much trouble to get my undivided attention."

Ha! As if she'd go to any trouble to get his attention, undivided or not. "If that was what I wanted, Mac, I'd have skipped out during the how-we-clean-the-horse's-teeth lessons and just invited you to go skinny-dipping with me at midnight."

That seemed to give him a moment's pause. "As I recall the last moonlight swim, I invited you."

"Oh, yes," she said irritably. "And as your memory of how things happened is so vastly superior to mine, that must be the way it was." Abbie lifted her chin, ready for a fight. "You couldn't be wrong."

His gaze cut to her, cut back to the road. "You want me to stop and let you out? It's a long walk back to the ranch, but I'll tell you right now I won't put up with this kind of antagonistic attitude at the show, and it's a hell of a lot farther to walk from there."

He accused her of malice aforethought and then warned her not to have a bad attitude. How had she ever found him evenly remotely attractive? But one glance reminded her of the way his whole visage warmed with a smile, of how his eyes smoldered when lit by passion and, God help her, she wished he would look at her that way again. Unbidden, she remembered the trust she'd placed in him the moment they met. Without question or hesitation. It had been a once-in-a-lifetime, struck-by-lightning experience, an inner knowing she'd never expected to happen to her, but she'd recognized in an instant that he was special in ways it would take her a lifetime to discover. Only she hadn't had a lifetime to give. She'd wanted independence, her first real job, a couple of years to get some living under her belt. Maybe it would have turned out differently if she'd stayed a few more hours that fateful morning-after, but probably not. He was born a prince and he saw her only as a wannabe princess, not as the woman she'd been that night in his arms. "I'm not walking back to the ranch," she assured him coolly. "And I'm not going to miss my very first horse show because you're an egotistical jerk with a persecution complex."

"Switching from defense to offense," he said with an aggravating know-it-all nod of his head. "Good thinking."

"Yes, and the weekend has barely even begun."

His smile was slightly more centered this time. "In that case, I suggest we call a truce until the show is behind us."

"A truce?" she repeated, certain she couldn't have heard that correctly.

"Pass the olive branch. Smoke the peace pipe. Bury the hatchet. Agree to disagree for the next forty-eight hours. Get along for the good of the team. Rise above the situation. Roll with the punches. Grin and bear it.'' His focus shifted momentarily from the highway to her, changed perceptibly from annoyance to conciliation. ''You know, a truce.''

She stared at his profile, figuring there was a loophole in there somewhere. ''You left out 'kiss and make up.'''

His gaze returned to her, full strength and potent. ''Is that what you want?''

Yes. Yes, she did. ''Of course not,'' she said. ''I just want a clear understanding of what I'm expected to concede in this truce.''

''Animosity, mainly. A horse show means tight schedules and tighter quarters. There's no time for arguments or hurt feelings. Everyone has to focus on the goal, and that means not adding more stress to a stressful event. My feelings about you, or yours for me, have no place at this show. So I'm asking if you can put your agenda aside for the next two days and let me concentrate on doing what I do best.''

''Bullying people into doing what you tell them?''

A muscle in his jaw flexed. ''Look, it's going to be a long weekend and I don't want to spend it fighting with you. This is the last time I'll ask—will you agree to call a truce until we get back to the ranch?''

''Wait a minute, let me get this straight. You're asking *me* to make peace with *you?*''

''Well, I'd ask the horses in the back, but I've already cut my deal with them. So, that just leaves you.''

She was curious. ''What sort of deal do you make with a horse?''

''I give a horse my full attention, put my confidence in his ability, and do my best not to get in the way when he's working. In return, he'll do his damnedest to give me whatever I ask of him.''

''Oh, I see, so you expect me to do whatever you ask, too.''

For a second, there was humor in the dark gaze that flickered to her and away. ''It'd make my life easier, that's for sure. I tend to be a bit uptight at shows, not my usual easygoing self. I don't want to spend what little time I get for reflection worrying about you.''

She arched a skeptical eyebrow. ''And how would that be different from the time you *don't* spend worrying about me now?''

''Look. Sometimes I might snap at people during a show and I don't want you to take it personally if I should snap at you, once or twice.''

Abbie liked the sudden hesitancy in his voice. The idea that maybe at least on some level, he did care what she thought of him. ''Okay, so you expect me to do whatever you ask and not take it personally when you're rude. What would I get in return for my generosity of spirit in granting you this truce?''

''Don't get cocky. I've already given you more hands-on instruction than I should have.''

''You can say that again.'' Abbie said, and laid her arms lightly across the bulge of belly that was their baby.

His expression darkened. ''That isn't what I meant and you know it.''

''You meant that I should be so appreciative of all the time you expended on me this week, I agree to anything just to make you happy.'' She lifted her shoulder in a careless shrug. "Sorry. Your happiness isn't high on my priority list."

"Fine," he snapped. "We'll forget about negotiating peace and I'll simply tell you how this weekend is going to go down. I'll show you where to sit to watch the show. You'll sit there and enjoy yourself, or not, as you choose. But you will stay away from the horses, and you will stay away from me. And that, Abbie, is not open for argument."

"Why didn't you just order me out of the truck before we left the ranch? You didn't have to bring me along if you were only going to treat me like a kid and make me sit in the stands the whole time."

"I figured as determined as you are, you'd just borrow a car and drive yourself. This way, at least, I can keep an eye on you."

"Which is what you've just said you don't want to have to spend a moment doing." She turned toward him, desperate to be allowed a small part in the weekend's activities. "I can be a help, Mac. I know I can. Even Livy said I caught on fast and the horses seemed to like me."

His sharp look cut through her persistence. "You're pregnant, Abbie. You have no business being anywhere near a horse."

"I'm not going to get on one and gallop around while doing side-to-side flips off the horse's back. I'll just hold the reins or help with the grooming or the costumes. I'll even clean their teeth, if that's what needs to be done."

"No," he said forcefully. "You don't know what can happen. The horses get nervous and excited at these shows, too. They get spooked more easily, take exception to strangers holding their halters, act out. You could get pulled off balance and take a fall. The horse could kick you. You, or your baby, could get hurt.''

''And you expect me to believe you care?''

''Of course, I care. Just because I don't believe it's my baby doesn't mean I wouldn't care if something happened to you, or to it.''

Suddenly furious, she doused him in chilly thought waves. ''Why did you bother teaching me anything, then? Why didn't you say you weren't willing to take the responsibility?''

''You said you wanted to learn. If I'd known you were plotting an all-out invasion, I'd have ordered you back to the office and out of my arena.'' His voice was agitated again. ''I don't know how you talked Jessica into helping you pull this one off, but I intend to set her straight about you the minute we get back.''

''Maybe I'll set her straight about you,'' Abbie said, stung into anger. ''Maybe I'll set the whole family straight.''

His gaze burned a path to hers. ''Don't threaten me, Abbie.''

She closed her eyes, suddenly weary of fighting a battle she didn't even want to win. ''All right,'' she said. ''I'll agree to your stupid truce.''

''A little late for that now. Not that you'd care. You probably get a perverse thrill just thinking you can keep me off-focus and out of the winner's circle.''

Her eyes flashed fire as they flew open. ''That isn't fair.''

''No, and it isn't fair that you connived and lied to

Jessie and probably every other member of my family, just so you could be here to irritate me in person, instead of from a distance.''

''You know what?'' She glared out the window because her eyes were brimming with hot tears. ''I'm going to sit right here the rest of the trip and irritate you by refusing to speak to you, again. How's that for a truce?''

''Couldn't ask for more,'' he said coolly, taking his cue and glaring out the windshield on his side of the truck cab.

OKAY, SO HE'D TRIED to take the high road and be nice to her, but she would have none of it. It had to be her way or no way. But what had she said, how many lies had she concocted, to draw Jess into her corner? Had Abbie come right out and voiced her claim that he was the father of her baby? Or had she merely implied and let his cousin's vivid imagination propel her into matchmaker mode? Mac didn't doubt that something—no, make that *someone*—had prompted Jessie into taking action. He knew that, even with her finely honed skill at manipulating others, Abbie couldn't have talked her way out of the office without Jess's cooperation and encouragement. But what did Jessie think would happen if she shoved Abbie into his path at every other turn? Spontaneous combustion? Reconciliation? And how could she know there was anything to reconcile unless Abbie had told her?

Which was what had to have happened. Abbie had skillfully let the information slip out that she and Mac had a one-night history. From there, Jessie would have leaped to the conclusion Abbie had wanted her to reach all along. Either that Mac was the father of the baby, as Abbie claimed. Or that he would rescue her and her illegitimate child from a desperate and dismal future. And either way, Jess was wrong. Wrong, wrong, wrong. He'd fallen in love with a manipulator once before. He knew their methods. He'd be crazy to overlook the obvious this time around just because he'd believed...hoped...she was different. She'd already proved she wasn't. He recognized trouble when he saw it coming at him, and Abbie was trouble. Why, she could have slept with a dozen men the night before the graduation party. Or all the nights leading up to it, for that matter.

His gut twisted with the irony. He'd fallen hard for her that night, had spent many nights since wondering if she could possibly be as beautiful, as smart, as genuine as she'd seemed in the few hours they'd shared. She was still beautiful. Even a glance in her general direction made him aware of the bounce in her sandy-brown hair, the classic lines of her profile, the full kiss-me invitation of her lips. She was obviously smart. Not only could she decipher some of the frustrating fractions involved in the business part of ranching, but she always seemed about two steps ahead of him in any conversation. Genuine? No, but if his perceptions weren't as sharp, he would most likely have taken her at her word and they'd be married by now.

Now, there was a scary thought. How easily she might have duped him, if only Gillian hadn't taught him all he ever needed to learn about women and their private agendas. Well, he'd be damned if he'd break

Abbie's declared truce of silence. Cold shoulder was more like it, but sooner or later on this four-hour trip to Dallas, a pregnant lady would need to stop to refresh herself. He'd bide his time, wait for her to ask him to stop, see how she felt about his very generous offer of a real truce then.

Hannah called for a halt at the next rest station and, without a word, Abbie slid out of the truck. Fifteen minutes later, Alex climbed into the truck cab and slammed the door. ''Abbie and Hannah sent me to ride with you, said they want to talk 'girl talk' for a while.''

Mac didn't say a word, just ground the gears as he shifted into drive and led the convoy back onto the highway.

AT FIRST, MAC WAS TOO BUSY to notice the sly looks and quickly averted grins, but gradually, as the horses were settled into their stalls, as the equipment was unpacked and squared away, and the empty trailers rattled off to the parking area, he became aware that he was the object of a playful speculation. He dismissed it as the sportive hijinks of athletes who were revved for competition, but when Alex slapped him on the back and said, ''Quick work, brother. I didn't think you liked her, but my wife tells me she figured out days ago that there was something going on between you two. Hannah is amazing, huh?'' Alex looked like a man who'd stumbled blindly into paradise. It was a look that had descended on him at his wedding, as he watched Hannah, in bridal white, walk up the aisle toward him. Mac had been awed at the time, but since then, he found himself growing a little impatient with all this newlywed bliss mumbo jumbo. Days like today he felt sure it had garbled his brother's brain cells. "What are you talking about?" he asked, pulling out a can of leather oil as he straddled a stool and prepared to give his saddle a touch-up. "You don't think just because Abbie rode with me for part of the trip that she and I, that the two of us are a...a couple, do you?"

"Well, I didn't think so, but when I heard about the sleeping arrangements, I figured maybe Hannah was right."

"What sleeping arrangements?" Mac sat straighter, his nerves on instant alert.

"Word is, you requested a double room and put Abbie down as the person who'd be sharing it with you. Everybody's talking about it."

Mac controlled his annoyance with considerable effort. He couldn't trust Abbie to act as if she had a grain of common sense. Apparently, he wasn't going to be able to let her out of his sight for fifteen minutes this whole weekend. "If she's registered as my roommate, then someone made a mistake. I hardly know the woman, why would I want to share a room with her? Plus she's pregnant."

Alex shrugged. "Hannah says women can have sex during pregnancy, right up till the final few weeks. And she is a doctor, so I guess she knows."

"She's a veterinarian," Mac said. "And I'm not having sex with Abbie. The room situation is a mixup, one I intend to straighten out right now."

"Give me that brush." Alex took over the task of polishing the saddle. "If it turns out the hotel's overbooked and there's not another room available, you might be able to bunk with Stanley, providing he doesn't already have a roommate. If worse comes to worst, I guess you can sleep on the floor in our room."

"I'm sure Hannah would not be thrilled with that arrangement," Mac said, grabbing his hat.

"Hannah, hell. I only offered because I knew you wouldn't take me up on it. This way I can still get credit for being a nice guy."

"If it comes to that, I'll sleep in my truck," Mac assured him, and headed out to see what Abbie had done now to further screw up his life.

WHEN HE FINALLY TRACKED her down, she was in the hotel restaurant with Livy, Hannah and a handful of other women, most of whom boarded horses at the Desert Rose and were here to ride in the show. "May I speak to you?" He leaned in to speak to Abbie, but spread his smile among the women assembled around the table. "In private, please?"

Abbie barely looked at him. "You heard about the mixup with the room, I take it."

"I heard," he said, careful to school any trace of annoyance out of his voice and expression. "And I'd like to talk to you about it."

"That won't be necessary," she said, her smile tight, her eyes refusing to meet his. "I handled it."

His temper flared, but he held on to his manners by sheer willpower. "Yes, I'm sure you did, which is why I'd prefer to have this discussion in private. If you wouldn't mind."

"Mac," Livy said brightly, missing the underlying thread of tension altogether. "Settle a bet. Do people in Balahar wear clothes like the costumes we wear in the Costume Class or not?''

He frowned and Livy apparently thought he didn't understand the question. ''What I mean,'' she tried to clarify, ''is do desert sheikhs really wear flowing robes and headpieces and glittery outfits when they ride their horses?''

''I don't know. Why don't you ask someone who's actually been there? Serena, for instance. Or my mother?'' He turned a more purposeful look to his quarry. ''Abbie? Could you come with me, please?''

Seated next to Olivia was a lanky brunette—Mac couldn't remember her name—who gave him a brilliant smile and scooted her chair over in invitation. ''We just ordered lunch,'' she said. ''Why don't you join us?''

It would serve Abbie right if he joined the circle and made her uncomfortable for a change, but he didn't have the time or the inclination. ''I'll only steal her away from you for a few minutes.'' With a display of charm, he included every one of the women at the table in his flashing grin. ''I promise to return her long before the food arrives. Now, if you'll excuse us...?''

He put his hand on the back of Abbie's chair, deciding he'd pick her up in it and carry her out to the lobby, if necessary. But she pushed away from the table with undisguised irritation. ''If I'm not back in ten minutes, you can all share my French fries, providing you make certain Mac picks up the check.'' They responded as if she'd made a joke, but there was an uncertain note in their laughter, as if the situation had just now struck them as odd. Mac didn't care what they thought. He reached a hand out to take her elbow, but she stiffened and swung away to avoid the touch. Then she walked ahead of him out of the restaurant and into the hotel lobby.

"You want to tell me what you think you're doing?" The question was out of his mouth almost before she wheeled to face him.

"I was about to have lunch before you so rudely interrupted. What do you think *you're* doing?" Her voice was quiet but deadly, and her eyes harbored a chill in which a snowflake would feel right at home.

"I intend to find out exactly what happened with the room."

"What happened is that someone registered us as roommates," she said matter-of-factly.

He was irritated all over again, mainly because her hair was attractively tousled and her cheeks were flushed with color and the soft pink overalls she was wearing over a flowered T-shirt made her look petite and feminine and as if she could use a man to protect her. The rounded bump of her pregnancy was hardly even noticeable. Her aggravation with him, however, would be clear as a bell to anyone who chanced to look in their direction. "How could anyone make that big a mistake?" he asked.

"I suppose it could have been a clerical error, but my best guess is that whoever made the reservations set it up that way."

"Funny," he said without humor. "That's exactly what I would have guessed."

"Imagine that. We agree on something."

"Only if you're being honest for a change and actually admitting you're responsible for the mixup."

Her lips tightened and her eyes glistened with true-blue disgust. "I knew you'd jump to that conclusion, Mac. That's why I didn't want to have this discussion. I told you I handled the situation. Why couldn't you just leave it at that and leave me alone?"

"Because next up on your scheming little agenda, I expect you're going to tell me the hotel is over-booked and we really have no choice except to share the room. After that, I'm guessing you'll be all blushes when anyone suggests we *enjoyed* our night together. From there, I'm not sure where you'd head, but I can assure you I'm not going to be tricked into marrying you no matter how many underhanded schemes you dream up."

Her eyebrows rose and he thought for a second her gaze would burn a hole in his forehead. "What makes you think I would ever want to marry you?"

Something in her voice cooled his temper, sent an icy chill skating along his spine. "Why else would you have shown up on my ranch in your condition?"

"Because my friend invited me to visit her, I had no place else to go, and this is the *condition* I'm in. I had no more idea it was also your ranch than you had that I was friends with your cousin." She stopped, pressed her lips together, as if to keep in words that still threatened to tumble out. "I think we've covered this ground before, so I'll just go on back and have my lunch."

"Whoa, there," he said as she started to turn and retreat. "There's still the little matter of where we'll be sleeping to clear up."

She paused, squared her shoulders and faced him once again. "Where I sleep is none of your business and I have absolutely no interest in where you sleep as long as it isn't in a bed with me. Been there, done that. Big mistake. It is true that the hotel had us booked into the same room, but I took care of it. They moved you to another room and put Livy in with me. Let's label it a clerical error and forget about it."

Her forceful denial was not only articulate but believable. He came within a split second of apologizing, but then he snapped to his senses. "But it wasn't a clerical error, Abbie, was it?"

She reached into her pocket and pulled out a cell phone no bigger than the palm of her hand. "Here." She thrust it toward him. "Call Jessica right now and let's get to the bottom of this great mystery. She'll be in the office. She was there when the reservations were made. Call her."

He wanted to back away from the phone, as if it were a time bomb set to explode. Which was silly. Jessica wouldn't lie to cover for Abbie. Jess was a Coleman and family was the bottom line. When push came to shove, she would be on his side. So why was he hesitating? "And what do you think she's going to tell me? That *she* set up the whole thing?"

Abbie's chin came up. "Call her," she challenged. "The phone's on. Punch in the office number and let's find out what she has to say."

She seemed so confident, so eager to prove he was in the wrong. He wanted to be suspicious of that, too, but now that he thought about it, he could see how his cousin might have engineered the roommate situation in the flawed hope something might come of it. Jessica was nothing if not a romantic at heart. "What exactly do you propose I ask her?"

Abbie shrugged. ''Ask her why she's trying to throw us together. Ask her what she's hoping to accomplish. Ask her if she's having delusions of being Cupid. Ask her anything you want. Just ask her and stop badgering me.''

Mac was on the fence, just about to jump off on the side of calling her bluff, when the phone vibrated in his hand and played a jangling snippet of a song. Startled, he looked at the electronic gadget tunefully requesting attention, but before he could hand the phone to Abbie, she snatched it out of his hand and took several hurried steps away from him before she stopped the ringing and put the phone to her ear. ''Hello?'' she said. With a turn and a lift of her shoulder, she signaled privacy, probably unaware she'd done so.

Mac was moving toward the registration desk, thinking he'd just make sure the rooms and roommates had been shuffled as she'd claimed, when he overheard her side of the conversation and caught her in a flat-out lie.

''Brad,'' he heard her say. ''Didn't I ask you not to call me until tonight?'' A pause. A strangled, gay little laugh. ''Of course, I'm still in the mountains. Yes, at the camp. Where else would I be?'' She glanced at Mac, and for a moment he held her gaze, but she quickly ducked her head, lowered her voice and shielded the rest of the conversation from him.

Brad. A man. Who wasn't supposed to call at this time of day. Who believed she was somewhere a long way from where she was. The Desert Rose was nestled right in the heart of Texas's hill country, but there wasn't a mountain within miles. And to his knowledge, no one had ever referred to the ranch as a camp. Abbie was lying to Brad, whoever he was. It was concrete proof that she was a liar, as he'd known from the start. He had every right to feel vindicated, justified and self-righteous.

So why was it he felt only sick at heart?

A HORSE SHOW WAS MORE WORK than Abbie could ever have imagined. The prelude to and aftermath of each individual event depended heavily on teamwork, and over the course of the weekend, she was surprised several times by the continuity of spirit that united the Desert Rose team. Never once did she see anyone shirk a responsibility, nor did she hear a note of complaint about doing what had to be done. Not that she did any of it. Mac made sure of that. True to his word, he banished her to a ringside seat, and although Olivia offered to sneak her behind the scenes, Abbie stayed where she was. It wasn't that she wouldn't have loved to do her part and take some small credit for the wins—and by Sunday, there were blue and purple ribbons all over the Desert Rose stalls—but she was so fascinated by the showmanship of all the horses and riders in the ring that she was almost grateful Mac had forced her to be merely an observer. Horses might represent a whole new world to her, but already she knew she would miss it terribly when she had to leave. And much as she hated to think about it, she knew her time at the Desert Rose ranch was nearly at an end.

Mac was suspicious of every move she made. Her brothers were growing restless with her continued insistence on being away for the whole summer. Even the baby was making his or her presence known, with unsettling kicks to remind her she couldn't keep postponing the decision to face her family and the future. When she got back to the ranch, she'd explain to Jessica that she couldn't stay, that she would, in fact, leave at the end of next week. Provided Mac didn't provoke her into an earlier departure.

A ripple of excitement swept the arena as the mare and foal competition began its final round. Abbie, and Hannah beside her, clapped long and loudly as Olivia entered the ring with Khalahari and Khalid. As if he believed the applause could only be for him, the dusky colt arched his neck proudly and pranced like a champion. "Look at him," Hannah said with a laugh. "Obviously, he believes the prize is his, even before the rest of the contestants have entered the ring. You've got to love his attitude. Seems to be prevalent in the Coleman men, as well."

"Do they always win?" Abbie asked, her eyes on Jabbar's prancing son, even if her question was basically about Mac.

"Well, 'always' is a hazy term, but they win far more often than not. When Alex, Cade or Mac is riding one of the Desert Rose stallions, it's practically written in the stars that they'll sweep the costume classes. There's something a little mystical about seeing any one of the brothers, garbed in the flashy costumes, astride a beautiful black Arabian." Hannah inhaled soulfully. "The first time I saw Alex on Jabar, I fell in love. I was probably eight at the time. One look and that was it for me. It took him considerably longer to realize I was even in the world, but he finally came around and realized I was a match made in heaven especially for him.'' She smiled, happiness shining like a vein of gold in her blue eyes.

Abbie felt a fleeting pang of regret that she'd missed out on such obvious bliss, but she dismissed it and agreed with Hannah's observation. ''The Coleman brothers are very handsome and the Desert Rose horses are exceptionally gorgeous.''

''It's more than that,'' Hannah said. ''I can't describe it, but it's really something to see. Wait until this afternoon when you can watch Mac. I wish you could see him riding Texas Heat or Dakar, but he's showing a young stallion called Sultan, this weekend. Not that the two of them won't be incredible to watch, but there's a big difference when the horse and trainer have worked together for years and have built up their rapport and trust in each other. Mac is a gifted trainer, though, and Sultan is coming along nicely. I expect they'll easily win their division.'' Hannah laughed. ''As you can tell, I'm not the slightest bit prejudiced in my predictions. Although, I'll confess, I wish Alex were riding. It's shameless of me, I know, but he really is the handsomest of the brothers.''

''I'd never argue with a new bride,'' Abbie said diplomatically. But when Mac rode into the showring a couple of hours later, she decided Hannah was wrong. Mac looked so handsome and sat the blue-black stallion with such confidence and pride, Abbie couldn't have said if there even were any other contestants in the arena. She couldn't tear her gaze from the sight of him, riding the circle of the ring on the beautiful horse. The costume was red and flowing, glittering with silvery designs. The headdress set off his dark Arabic features, and only the firm line of his jaw bespoke his fierce concentration on the spirited stallion he rode. When he urged Sultan forward to claim the grand prize, Abbie was surprised only to realize she was still breathing in and breathing out at a regular rhythm.

"Flat steals your breath away, doesn't it?" Hannah nudged her and Abbie nodded, still mesmerized as Mac and Sultan took a victory lap around the ring. "I know how you feel. It's hard to keep in mind that he's just a man on a horse."

Abbie sighed and repeated, "Just a man on a horse."

OLIVIA WAS KEYED UP from her win in the mare and foal division and returned to the subject again and again on the trip home. Abbie, who had asked for the shotgun seat in Livy's truck, listened absently as the details were replayed yet again. "I told Mac he could do it," she said, and Abbie smiled, as if she hadn't heard this at least once already. "Khalid is going to break every record out there, you wait and see. Mac wasn't sure he was ready, but I knew he'd settle down the minute he realized there was an audience. For a four-month-old colt, he has a lot of presence, don't you think?" Livy was too excited to wait for an answer. "I'm predicting he's going to win so many ribbons in the next few years, they'll have to make up whole new divisions for him to enter. He's going to make every other Arabian colt look like a slug. I told Mac he was ready for this." She slapped the steering wheel with the palm of her hand. "Mac wasn't sure, but I knew. I just knew." She sobered for a half a second. "You don't think Mac was upset, do you?"

"Upset?" Abbie repeated, hoping no one—and especially not impressionable Olivia—had noticed the tension between her and Mac. "I can't imagine why he'd be upset when you won your division."

A smile flashed in Livy's violet eyes and high spirits returned to carry the day. "You're right, Abbie," she continued. "Mac asked me to work with Khalid because I bonded with the little guy right off. And we won, so why should he be upset?" She grinned at Abbie across the front seat of the truck. "I mean, he won his class, too."

Abbie nodded and wished a couple of things. One, that she had as much enthusiasm for life as Livy. And two, that someday she could feel as completely competent in her work as Livy felt in hers. Olivia had a gift, and whether she realized it or not, the knowledge of it invested her with authority. Abbie didn't feel she had a gift for anything except getting herself into impossible predicaments. She'd wanted to be a teacher from as far back as she could recall, but now that she'd been summarily dismissed from Miss Amelia's Academy, she'd probably be lucky ever to teach anywhere again. Well, maybe that was a bit too pessimistic, but even if she had another teaching position lined up, there was the baby to think about, the logistics of child care and quality time, and time to grade papers, prepare lessons, be the kind of teacher she wanted to be. So before she could even find out if she had a future in her chosen field, her long-awaited independence had taken a swan dive and landed her in this pickle of pickles. She'd made one impulsive choice, taken one foolish chance, and now her future was framed within the parameters of a much more daunting career—motherhood.

"Maybe he's not upset, but I still think Mac was a little off this weekend," Livy continued. "I mean, didn't you think he seemed tense the whole time? Worried, maybe? Well, you probably don't know him well enough to tell, but something was bothering him. Sultan was really showing out today, stuff Mac never lets any horse get away with. I think he was distracted."

"Sultan won," Abbie pointed out, knowing she sounded somewhat defensive. "Mac can't have been too preoccupied."

Livy's sharp glance darted to Abbie. "Probably only somebody like me, who's worked with him a lot, would have noticed anything. And I wasn't saying that whatever it was kept him from giving an outstanding performance. He just seemed off to me, a bit off balance in his concentration, that's all, and I just can't help wondering what—or who—is on his mind."

Abbie could have provided a list of reasons Mac seemed "off" in Livy's words. A list beginning and ending with her. She figured if Mac was in any way, shape or form unhappy with his and Sultan's accomplishment in the ring, it would wind up being her fault. She was a distraction. She had made him angry. She had put a burr under the saddle blanket. She had messed up the hotel reservations and that meant he had ended up on a lumpy mattress, or been kept awake all night by noisy neighbors, or couldn't sleep for worrying how she would try to trick him into marriage—or all of the above. There was no way for her to win with Mac. She should just get out at the next rest stop and thumb a ride to Arkansas or Kalamazoo. But she didn't want to go either place. She wanted one more week to prepare her speech, to beef up her resolve, to be alone with the knowledge of her baby's existence.

Well, Mac knew, but he didn't count. In fact, she didn't know why she cared if she was a distraction to him. He'd won, for Pete's sake, and even if he'd done it only because he looked the part of a desert prince, he still had no reason to complain. She'd asked nothing of him up to this point. And she wouldn't in the future, either. All she wanted was to be with her friend, to have just another week in which to gather strength before she faced her family. If that kept him *off,* well, too bad. She had done nothing wrong, unless she counted falling for a Texas sheikh and failing to realize he was just a man on a horse.

Chapter Six

"It's clear as glass, she planned the whole thing, beginning to end. And I don't see why I should have to be the bad guy just because she's manipulated her way into being Jessie's friend." Mac braced his arms on the top rail of the pasture gate and set the sole of his boot on the bottom rail as he concluded the entire, unexpurgated story of his involvement with Abbie. Beside him, Cade assumed the same position, one foot braced against the bottom rail, arms propped across the top, his gaze—like Mac's—centered on the mares and their foals grazing contentedly on the summer grasses. There was a sense of wholeness when he was with Cade, something about the alignment of their individual stances, the tilt of their hats, the way they looked at things, the knowledge that someone understood him about as well as he understood himself. It was their twinship that made them not only physically identical down to the last hair on their heads, but also gave them the shared history that fostered a special insight each into the other. There wasn't any other person Mac wanted to talk to about Abbie and her baby. No one else he trusted enough to confess the whole sordid story to. He knew Cade would see things his way, or show him where he lacked perspective. For good or ill, Cade would tell him the truth. "I think," Mac continued, "that I should tell Jess what her friend is really like and insist she be the one to ask Abbie to leave the ranch."

"Is that what you want to happen? For Abbie to just go away?" Cade paused, then specified the answer he expected. "Truth."

"Yes," Mac said without hesitation, then realized with a jarring twist in his gut that he really wasn't going to be any happier when she was gone. "No. I don't know. She's a liar, a schemer. Worse even than Gillian was. I shouldn't give a solitary damn if she disappeared from the face of the earth. But right now, the truth is, I feel this crazy impulse to protect her, to step in and save her from the mess she's made and I'm really not sure how I'm going to feel once she's gone."

"You want my opinion?" Cade asked.

"No, I want Stanley's," Mac replied dryly. "Of course, I want your opinion. Otherwise we wouldn't be here talking about this. I wouldn't have just confessed to you my part in this soap opera or told you how really stupid I was for falling for her innocent facade in the first place."

"You're in love with her," Cade said confidently. "It's the only explanation."

Mac turned his head and stared at his brother. "This is no time for jokes," he said.

"Consider the possibility, Mac. You fell in love with her back in December, you've thought about little else except her ever since—your words, not mine—and when she showed up here at the ranch, you panicked and started imagining it was all a setup to trap you into marriage and fatherhood. With what Gillian did to you, that knee-jerk reaction is—''

''Knee-jerk?''

''That's what I said,'' Cade continued calmly. ''You reacted to Abbie's announcement about the baby by jumping to a perfectly understandable conclusion, considering your history with the last woman—actually, the only other woman you ever fell hard for. But that doesn't mean you automatically jumped to the right conclusion.''

''I'm not wrong about this, Cade.'' But even as he said it, Mac knew he wanted his brother to convince him he might be. ''And I am not in love with Abbie. I slept with her once five months ago. I'm pretty sure that qualifies as lust, not love.''

''If it had been nothing more than lust, you'd have forgotten about it the next day when she skipped out. And by your own admission, you didn't. Love can happen that fast,'' Cade assured him. ''Look at Serena and me. One minute we're married due to a cultural misunderstanding and the next thing you know, I'm head over heels for her. When it's the right woman, Mac, logic really plays no part in it.''

''If this is all the help you're going to be, I think I'll just ride out and have a talk with a scrub oak.''

''You're not listening to me, buddy. You're in denial.''

''And you're still in that annoying stage of romance where you think everyone is or should be in love with everyone else. You're wearing rose-colored glasses, Cade. Probably will be for months to come. You and Alex. What a time for both my brothers to be so besotted with their respective brides that they haven't a sensible word to say to me."

"The word I have for you is, give it a chance." Cade pulled down the brim of his hat and took his boot off the bottom rail, breaking the syncronicity as his gaze shifted toward the property line and the green acres on the other side. "I've asked Nick Grayson and Uncle Randy if Coleman-Grayson Corporation will help Serena and me buy the McGovern place. It'll give the ranch room for expansion and give me a little more privacy with my wife. If McGovern agrees to sell at our offering price, and Nick thinks he will, we could be moving in by September."

"That's good news," Mac said, honestly pleased by his twin's plan but wishing he had a better answer for his own situation. "That way you and Serena can make a home of your own and you can still be home."

"Exactly what we thought, although I have promised Serena we'll spend at least a month or two in Balahar every year. She's excited about that." Cade continued to look across the distant fence that divided the Desert Rose from the McGovern property. "Okay. Here's my best advice, Mac. Up to now, you've tried ignoring Abbie. You've tried confronting her with her lies. You've tried to force her to admit she's exactly like Gillian. I'm not saying she isn't lying, Mac. I'm only saying you ought to consider the idea that maybe she isn't."

"She is," Mac protested, trying to keep his rock-solid belief in her duplicity from crumbling like sandstone. "We spent one night together, Cade. One night. We used protection against pregnancy—I wasn't completely blindsided by lust—and it just seems too strange to me that five months later she turns up pregnant...here, of all places."

"It is an odd set of circumstances, Mac, but what if everything she told you is the truth? Stranger things have happened."

"Lightning doesn't strike twice."

"Sorry, brother, but even science isn't going to back you up on that angle. It's true you got burned pretty badly by Gillian, but that doesn't mean Abbie is just like her. It just means you're more suspicious than maybe you ought to be."

"I have a right to be suspicious," Mac argued. "Her story doesn't hold up. Haven't you noticed how she carries that little cell phone everywhere she goes? Never lets it out of her sight, and she gets mysterious phone calls all the time from some guy. I've heard her talking to him. Now tell me there's not something downright sneaky about that. About her."

"Maybe," Cade said. "And maybe not. If Abbie is as devious and sly and downright sneaky as you're convinced she is, then it's going to come as a big surprise to everyone except you. Jessie adores Abbie. Serena likes her. Hannah likes her. Aunt Vi and Mom like her. Every other male on this ranch breaks out in a grin anytime she glances in their direction, and that includes me. Why don't you stop torturing yourself with trying to figure out how she's like Gillian and start trying to figure out how she's different? What if Abbie actually is the special person you first thought she was? What if you tried to have an honest conversation with her about what happened and what she expects from you instead of baiting her at every turn and waiting for her to make a mistake?''

Mac frowned. ''I can't just pretend to believe her all of a sudden.''

''No, but think about it this way. What would happen if you suddenly discovered solid evidence that she'd been telling the truth all along?''

Mac thought about that. Remembered Abbie's sleek body beside him, naked on the bed, beneath him, welcoming him inside. Remembered how he'd fallen in love with her laugh, how he'd felt wrapped in warmth just hearing it. Remembered how lost he'd felt when he realized she was gone without a trace. ''If I thought for a minute she was telling the truth, I suppose I'd have to marry her.''

Cade grinned. ''That's it, then. Love in the first degree.''

Mac offered no answering grin in return. ''That is no help, Cade. It doesn't even make sense.''

''Okay, then, let's put this on a level you'll understand. Come with me.'' He led the way to the barn, his gaze searching the ground, until he found what he wanted—a wayward stem of hay. Holding it out, he said, ''We'll draw straws. You get the short straw, you have the talk with Jessie and get Abbie evicted. I draw the short straw, you take my advice and spend time—and I do mean quality time—being nice to Abbie. Agreed?''

Mac studied the piece of straw. "You want to draw straws to decide whether or not I have to follow your dumb advice? You're not just making another stupid joke?"

In answer, Cade snapped the straw in two, showed Mac that they were of different lengths, then put them in his palm and put his hands behind his back. When he brought his hands forward again, the ends of the straw extended out evenly. "Take your pick, twin."

"This is ridiculous," Mac said, eyeing the straws.

"Afraid you'll lose?"

"How much quality time are we talking about?"

"How much can you stand?"

"An hour, maybe."

"A week," Cade countered.

"A day."

Cade shook his head. "Today's Monday. You have to give it at least through this coming weekend."

"That's six whole days."

"Yeah, plus what's left of this one. You're not chicken, are you, Mac?"

What was he worried about? Mac wondered. He'd won at this game before. "You're on," he said, and chose his playing piece...and came up the loser.

ABBIE EXPECTED THE WORST when Mac slipped into the seat beside her at dinner. His nearness unnerved her. His pleasant "Mmm, this looks good, doesn't it?" made her edgy. His under-his-breath suggestion to her of "You're going to want an extra helping of that casserole, trust me" knotted her healthy appetite into a lump of anxiety. When he asked, solicitously, if Jessie had given her the day off so she could recover from the demands of her weekend at the horse show, then accused his cousin of overworking the best help she was ever likely to get, Abbie couldn't imagine what mischief he was plotting. But when he smiled at her—a really bone-melting smile—over the bowl of mashed potatoes, she knew that whatever he was doing, it was going to get her into trouble.

He was going to tell the whole table she was here under false pretenses. He was going to lull her into a false security, then pull out the guns of accusation and shoot holes in any defense she offered. He was going to embarrass and humiliate her in front of his family. He was going to…

He did nothing, as it turned out. He made several pleasant comments to her over the course of dinner and went out of his way at every turn to include her in whatever discussion he had with anyone else. As dessert—Ella's fantastic blackberry cobbler topped off with homemade vanilla ice cream—was being passed out, Alex rose and tapped a spoon against his water glass. When the murmur of conversation died back, he cleared his throat and placed his hand on Hannah's shoulder. "I have an announcement," he said. "Hannah and I are…" His face creased with a grin. "She's pregnant, and the doctor said today he thinks it's twins!"

"Congratulations!" Cade was the first one to jump up to slap his older brother on the back and give Hannah a kiss on the cheek, but Mac was right behind him and Jessica followed close on their heels. Rose and Vi seemed a little misty-eyed, and Ella was so excited she let the ice-cream scooper drip all over the dining room floor while she hugged first Alex, then Hannah, then her own husband, Hal, for good measure.

After that, there were periodic whoops of laughter, a bubble of excited chatter that rose and fell...and rose again. Through it all, for the rest of the evening, Mac stayed at Abbie's side. He told her how he and Cade had prompted Alex into courting Hannah, suggested that if Abbie still wanted to learn about the Arabians, he'd be happy to continue her lessons, asked if she wanted more cobbler or ice cream, offered to get her a footstool, a pillow to place behind her back, even suggested a glass of milk would be good for her and help her sleep soundly. By the time she pleaded that it was well past her bedtime and time for her to go upstairs, she half expected him to insist upon tucking her into bed and reading her a bedtime story. Arabian Nights, probably.

She fell asleep thoroughly confused and with her suspicions in a complete muddle. What in the heck was he up to?

MAC HADN'T THOUGHT being nice to Abbie could be so easy. He'd refused to think about how easily Cade's advice could backfire, and pulled out all the charm he could muster. For the next two days, he sat next to her at dinner. He made sure she was included in his conversations. He smiled. He asked her opinion. He smiled some more. The only thing he didn't do, didn't dare do, was touch her in even the most casual gesture. For one thing, he didn't want her to slap his hand, and for another, he was afraid of what would happen if he did. Touching Abbie might tempt him to do something more than just touch her, kiss her, perhaps. And that could ignite the embers of a physical attraction sizzling just beneath the surface. And that would spell disaster in more ways than one. He could wake up and find himself not only married to her, but an expectant father, as well.

Oh, it wasn't that he suddenly believed her story and accepted Cade's love-at-first-sight theory. He didn't. Not at all. But he felt it was important to maintain at least one line he wouldn't cross, some measure of just how far he was willing to go to prove his brother was wrong. Abbie was a liar. The baby was not, could not, be his. But he'd agreed to play the game and it wouldn't kill him to pretend to have a change of heart for the rest of the week, just so long as he kept his hands off her. And who knew? Maybe Abbie would respond by letting down her guard. Maybe she'd decide, all on her own, to abandon her plans and leave the ranch. Maybe she'd get careless and he could catch her in her web of lies. Maybe, nothing would change.

Or maybe he'd discover that Cade was right.

Mac didn't want to think about that possibility, but since his talk with his twin, the idea that Abbie's baby could also be his baby had circled through his thoughts a million times. If there was one chance in ten million, even one in a billion, he had to consider what he'd do, although he knew in his heart the answer was a foregone conclusion. If a paternity test proved her baby was a Coleman, he would marry Abbie. And he would do it knowing that by insisting on that tangible, scientific proof, he had lost any hope of ever having her respect, trust, love or forgiveness.

MAC WAS HEADED into the kitchen, thinking that might be where Abbie had disappeared to after dinner. He was halfway there when he heard his mother's laugh and her voice confessing, "When I was pregnant with the twins, there were a couple of months when I cried at the slightest thing. One time, Ibrahim offered me anything I wanted—jewelry, clothes, a pet monkey, a trip home to visit Randy, anything I wanted, if I'd just stop crying."

Abbie's laugh rang out, along with Aunt Vi's and Hannah's. "He offered you a monkey?" Aunt Vi's voice was pitched high on the wave of her laughter. "As if that would make you feel better. Men are so inept when it comes to knowing how to deal with a pregnant woman. Why, when I was pregnant with Jessica, Randy used to watch me as if he thought I might suddenly pick up the BarcaLounger and throw it at him."

Mac turned to escape, knowing he didn't need to hear this, but then Abbie voiced a hesitant question and he felt it might be in his own best interests to eavesdrop a little longer. "Do you think it's the crying, or the idea they might be held responsible for it that upsets the men?" she asked.

"It's the tears," Rose said confidently. "Ibrahim was the king of Sorajhee. He could do almost anything by saying 'Make it so,' but he couldn't do a single thing to stop his pregnant wife from crying her eyes out.''

''Men always want to fix things,'' Aunt Vi added her agreement. ''If you're mad, they tell you why you shouldn't be. If you're frustrated with a project, they believe the answer is to finish the project for you. Men think if their wife is happy, they did something right and deserve a pat on the back. If she's not happy, they assume something must be wrong and it's their duty to find out what it is and beat the problem to a pulp. But if a woman is crying, men are helpless and all they can think to do is try to make it stop, or better yet, prevent it from starting in the first place.''

''I guess they're afraid the crying will go on and on endlessly and they'll feel more and more helpless.'' Hannah's voice added to the discussion. ''The doctor told me today to expect some mood swings and some teary moments, but I'm so happy about being pregnant, it's hard to imagine I'd ever cry because of it.''

''Crying doesn't mean you're unhappy,'' Aunt Vi assured her. ''It's just that the hormones in your body are going haywire and you can't help it.''

''It's strange,'' said Abbie's voice again, and Mac leaned in, listening even harder than before. ''These past five months have not been easy, but I haven't experienced much in the way of mood swings. Even when I got fired from a job I loved, I didn't shed a single tear.''

''You got fired?'' Hannah asked. ''I can't imagine why. Jessie says you can work circles around anyone else she knows.''

"It wasn't that I didn't do my job," Abbie said. "It was because I'm unmarried and pregnant."

"What?"

"They can't do that!"

"That's illegal."

"It's an exclusive private school for young women and it is in the contract I signed that I agreed to keep my behavior as a model for my students. So I don't really blame the administration, although they could have been a little nicer about the whole thing. But even when all that was going on, I didn't cry. Didn't even want to. Then the day before I came here, I was watching an old episode of *I Love Lucy* and suddenly I was sobbing. I cried and cried and I couldn't stop it. Then suddenly, it was over. No warning either way."

"That's just the way I remember it, too," Aunt Vi concurred. "One minute you're fine, the next minute you're flooding ocean city."

Hannah laughed. "I can't wait to tell Alex what he has to look forward to."

"Oh, don't tell him, honey," Aunt Vi advised. "Let him muddle through just like every other guy has had to do since Adam worried over Eve."

"You can warn him," Rose said. "But I don't think it'll make a bit of difference. When the tears start, he'll be as helpless as his father was with me. Don't worry. Alex will survive."

"I'm sure he will." Hannah sounded as if she was certain of it. "But I want him to enjoy these next few months as much as I intend to. We'll all hope that nothing happens to really upset my apple cart."

"You're right." Abbie's voice again. "Imagine what could happen if the mood swings and something really upsetting happened all at once."

"That could scare every man on this place so bad they might all head for the hills. Course, there are days when I wouldn't mind that a bit!" Aunt Vi said, laughing. In a moment, the other women were laughing, too.

Then, a chair scraped and Mac decided he did not want to get caught eavesdropping on that conversation. It might upset the expectant mothers—well, one of them, anyway—and he definitely did not want to be responsible for setting off the biggest cryfest this side of the Rio Grande.

"WANT TO GO FOR A WALK down to the dock?"

Startled, Abbie blinked and looked up into Mac's face. "A w-walk?" she repeated, certain she must have heard wrong. "To the d-dock?"

Mac nodded, solemnly. "If you care...to take a dare, we can walk...to the dock." His singsong rhyme teased her, toyed with her anxiety, but it was the warmth in his smile that put her heart at war with her head. "I will swear...it's just for air, but if you'd rather...I can..." He stopped, laughed. "Sorry, I don't have a clue what rhymes with *rather.* Will you come with me anyway?"

Okay, so he wanted to get her out of the house and yell at her or something. For three whole days now, he'd been nice as pie. He'd given her more attention, paid her more compliments than she'd ever received from anyone—with the exception of her brothers—

and generally acted as if he wanted to be friends. She still hadn't a clue what was behind this transformation, but she had a strong suspicion it wasn't going to last. "Sure," she said, and rose from the sofa. "If we're going to swim, though, you should get your denim shirt."

The corners of his mouth curved in a softer, somehow more genuine, smile. "Sorry, but this time you'll have to provide your own swimsuit."

The look in his eyes felt intimate, as if he were inviting her for more than a walk, as if he thought *rather* might be made to rhyme with *kiss.* "I don't feel like swimming tonight," she said crisply, and stepped out ahead of him.

"Walking's good." He followed her from the television and rec room where various members of the family and staff gathered after supper. He held open the door that led onto the courtyard and closed it as he followed her through. "I like a good walk after a good meal. What about you?"

She peered at him in the gathering dusk, genuinely perplexed by his new attitude. "I enjoy walking," she agreed. "I can't help thinking, though, that this must be how Little Red Riding Hood felt when she met up with the wolf on the road to her grandmother's house."

Mac grinned. "You think I have wicked designs on your basket of goodies?"

"Yes," she said simply. "I'm thinking you lured me out here so you could stuff me in a box and mail me to Timbuktu."

"Nah. I'd have to look up the zip code and it's just too nice a night to spend with my head in a book."

"It is nice out. The temperature feels like it's still on the high side of eighty, but it's not bad."

"There's always a breeze off the lake." His hand touched her elbow to turn her toward the dock, but then dropped quickly away. "Come on. I'll race you."

"That wouldn't be much of a contest. You could win in a walk."

"Or you could win in a waddle."

Her face fell in an avalanche of dismay. She couldn't help it. "Do I really waddle?"

He turned, started to put his hands on her shoulders, then took a step back. But oddly enough, his expression stayed disarmingly tender. "No, of course, you don't. It was just a dumb joke. A really dumb, bad joke."

She looked into his eyes and was embarrassed at how much she wanted him to kiss her, hold her, crush her against his chest. "You're just saying that to make me feel better. I knew it. I waddle."

"If I wanted to make you feel better, I'd apologize for being such a jerk the day you arrived, and for a few days afterward."

She blinked. Her heart stopped, sped off again in a wishful *thud-thud, thud-thud.* "If I didn't know better, I'd think you swapped places with your twin and that he's the one who invited me out for a walk and who's been unnervingly nice to me all week long."

Mac cocked his head to the side. "Do you know better, Abbie?"

"There might be some circumstances in which you could fool me with that kind of switch, but offhand, I can't think of any."

He didn't bother to hide his surprise. "And how can you be so certain of who I am, and who I'm not?"

She couldn't tell him how she knew. It had been stupid even to admit she could tell the difference. "I don't want to tell you," she said honestly, and moved away from him, down the slope to the dock.

He caught up with her in one long stride. "Even Aunt Vi still sometimes mistakes me for Cade or Cade for me. And if we're really trying, we can hoodwink practically anyone. So why do you think you can tell the difference?"

She stopped halfway down the pier, braced both hands on the railing and breathed deeply of the fragrant air. "This is such a beautiful place. If I lived here, I'd build a house right over there, so I could look out at the lake every morning and every night." She felt a change in him and realized how that had sounded. Proprietary. Grasping. Exactly the way he believed her to be. Sighing, she decided to try to explain. "I didn't mean I intend to live here," she began. "I only meant that I...oh, never mind. You won't believe me, anyway."

He was quiet for a moment, his hands folding over the top of the dock rail as he looked at the dark guest house just visible on the north side of the lake. "I'd like to ask you something, Abbie." His voice was husky now, no trace of a smile anywhere in the words. "That night, the first time we met, was it as breathtaking as I remember? Or was it just the circumstances?''

A whole shower of memories washed over her, drowning her in remembered sensations. If this was a setup, if he intended to lash out with disbelief when he heard her answer, she would never, ever forgive him. ''It was better than breathtaking, Mac. It was better than the best night of my entire life.''

He was still for a moment, staring past her at the water. ''So why were you gone when I woke up?''

''I had a prior commitment.''

''A commitment that precluded leaving me a name, an address? I'd have been happy with just a promise to meet again at the same time, same place, next year.''

She could almost believe she'd hurt him, which she'd never, ever meant to do. ''I'm sorry. I wanted a night of mystery and passion. I didn't think about the consequences.''

''And now?'' he asked.

''I think about the consequences every day.''

Mac stood apart from her, silent, contemplative, for so long she feared he'd forgotten she was there. Then he turned and, as if he was about to touch a glowing-hot coal, he reached out and placed his hand on the bulge of her tummy. ''A baby,'' he said. ''That's a lot of consequences to think about all by yourself.''

She laid her hand over his and looked up into his eyes. ''I'm not asking you to share the responsibilities, Mac. I didn't come here to ask you for anything. Please believe me.''

He answered by turning his hand until he was palm

to palm with hers. Then he drew their conjoined hands down and around her, pulling her closer to him at the same time he tipped up her chin with his other hand. "I'd like to, Abbie," he whispered. "I'd really like to." Then his lips came down to close over hers and the sensations flooding her were suddenly real and not just remembered.

His kiss was tender tonight, unlike the anger-charged embrace her first night at the ranch. Where he'd been seeking an answer then, this time he seemed to be asking a question. The pressure of his kiss parted her lips and his tongue teased hers with a sensuous caress. Her knees turned to mush, as did the protests that flickered weakly in her brain before succumbing to the pleasure. She really had no choice but to lean into him, to accept what he offered, to realize that their chemistry was a powerful combination. The taste, the feel of him was familiar, despite the months of separation, and Abbie wondered why that didn't seem strange to her, why being in his arms felt so much like being home. She'd been with Mac once and yet she knew things about him it should have taken her years to learn. Like knowing the slight tremor in his lips meant he was exercising a willful restraint. Like knowing he wasn't conscious of the way his finger stroked her chin during the kiss. Like knowing he wanted her as much as he ever had and was still reluctant to admit it. Like knowing that if she asked for more, either by word or deed, he would withdraw. This kiss was a test, somehow, and try as she might, Abbie couldn't think of any way she could pass.

But in a moment, miraculously, it seemed she had. The kiss melted into scattered caresses across her nose, her forehead, her eyelids. His arms tightened around her. His breath blew past her ear in a shaky, sensuous relief. "Abbie," he whispered. "I'm not sure how this is going to work out, but—"

Her phone rang. From the back pocket of her maternity-banded jeans, the cell phone jangled a rude and inopportune summons. She thought about reaching back and turning it off. She thought about snatching it out of her pocket and tossing it and its annoying rattle into the lake. She thought about telling Mac to hold on to the words he'd been about to say while she gave the phone a proper burial at sea. But in the end, she knew the moment was ruined already, so as Mac stepped back, looking pale and as if he'd just had a narrow escape, she reached for the phone and answered her brother's call.

MAC LEANED against the dock rail and tried to look as if he wasn't interested in Abbie's phone conversation. She was turning him into a compulsive eavesdropper, it seemed. But he couldn't help but listen to her side of the phone call and if it helped him figure out her line of attack, the end would justify the means, wouldn't it? On the other hand, he was obligated because of his agreement with Cade to do as his twin had suggested and keep an open mind about interpreting what the conversation might mean.

"Hello," she said for openers, and Mac decided there was nothing sinister or sneaky about that.

"I know I said I'd call at seven, but I told you it

could be later, too.'' Her tone was impatient, but also conciliatory, as if she were sorry she hadn't called at seven, but annoyed to be asked about it.

''I was busy,'' she said. There was a definite note of frustration in her voice, possibly a thread of affection, too. No, he'd imagined the affection. Definitely, no affection.

''I'm working. Yes, as a counselor.''

Okay, so he had to call that one a lie. Unless she was a certified counselor and considered talking to him as work. There, Mac thought. That was incredibly open-minded.

''Didn't I just say that?''

From her side of the conversation, it sure sounded like an escalating argument. Not the furious kind of argument he'd had with her several times since her arrival, but the less aggressive kind of argument where she didn't want to do whatever the person at the other end of the line wanted or expected her to do. A tug-of-war kind of argument. That seemed a fair and unbiased assessment of what he was hearing. ''No,'' she was saying. ''No, this isn't a good time. I can't talk right now.''

Suspicion reared its head. That had to mean she didn't want Mac to hear what she had to say. On the other hand, a desire for privacy was perfectly normal. That, in itself, wasn't necessarily suspicious. Score three for being open-minded.

''I'm exactly where I told you I'd be, Brad.''

Brad. The same guy who'd phoned her at the restaurant. She didn't seem any happier to hear from him tonight, either. Although that could be because she'd been right in the middle of kissing another man, weaseling her way around his defenses, insinuating herself back into his good graces, planning how to turn…

Whoa, Mac reminded himself. Open mind. Keep an open mind. Maybe Brad was just a jerk who called at times she'd rather he didn't. But if that were true, why didn't she just turn off the phone?

Her voice suddenly rose with distress. "Why did you do that? I asked you to only use the cell phone number. You had no business at all to go calling Directory Assistance."

Mac frowned. Brad could be her accomplice. Or simply someone who didn't know where she was.

"Yes," she said on a long and defeated sigh. "I know there's not a Camp Two by Two in the Pocono Mountains or anywhere else in the northeast United States." A pause, then a more agitated, "Because I wanted to be alone and, no, I am not going to tell you where I am. You'd just show up here and cause trouble for me and I don't need any help with that!" Her voice shook like a willow in a windstorm and Mac turned toward her, no longer caring if she knew he'd been listening in. "Yes, I'm upset," she said. "I'm doing my best to—" her voice broke "—to take care of…of…" Her voice trailed away entirely, giving way to a sniff that could only mean tears were close behind.

Brad, whoever the hell he was, had done about enough damage in one phone call. There was no reason for the guy to make her cry. What if this coincided with one of those hormonal mood swings? That would be bad. That would be very bad. Mac took two strides to reach her. With one hand he grasped her shoulder and pulled her gently but firmly against him, then he quickly slipped the phone out of her hand and put it to his ear. ''Look, *Brad,*'' he said, ignoring Abbie's sudden, horrified gasp. ''You've upset Abbie and in her condition, she may start crying and never be able to stop.''

With a strangled yelp, Abbie grabbed for the phone, but Mac evaded her attempt to reclaim it—he was doing his best to save her from the insensitive jerk, dammit—and continued talking. ''She doesn't want to talk to you anymore right now, so I'm turning off this phone and she can call you back when and if she wants to.''

There was a long pause and then a man's voice, rough with worry, asking, ''Who the hell is this?''

Mac saw no reason not to tell him. ''Coleman. Mac Coleman.'' Then he terminated the call with relish and turned off the phone altogether, feeling a bit proud at his quick thinking.

But when he looked to Abbie, expecting at least a hint of gratitude for his rescue, he saw the sag in her shoulders, the dejection in the lowering of her chin, the awful dismay in her eyes. ''I wish you hadn't done that,'' she said. ''I really wish you hadn't done that.''

''Don't tell me you were enjoying talking to that guy.'' Mac wasn't sure what she thought he'd done, but he'd certainly expected her to be happier about it. ''He was upsetting you.''

''Yes,'' she said. ''He does that on a regular basis. They all do.''

"There's more than one?"

"Four, altogether. Each one as bad as the next."

Mac thought fast. Four men. A gang. And somehow Abbie was mixed up with them. "Why were they calling you?"

"To make sure I'm all right."

"And at the camp in the mountains," he suggested, trying hard to keep an open mind, "where you told them you were."

"It's complicated," she said, then sighed. "I really don't want to talk about this. It's bad enough that you told them…oh, well, never mind. It can't be helped now."

"I'm sorry," he said, although it irritated him to have to say it. "I thought I was helping."

"I know you did. Maybe it's best this way. My decision is made for me. And I was going to leave in a few days, anyway."

"Leave?"

She almost smiled. "You've been trying to get rid of me ever since I got here, Mac. Don't tell me you thought I'd just stay on indefinitely."

"I thought the past few days might have changed your mind about what I wanted."

"The past few days, while much more pleasant than the previous week, have only convinced me that you decided to try a different—and admittedly—nicer line of defense. I know you won't believe this, either, but I never intended to stay at the Desert Rose more than a couple of weeks. Three, at the outside."

So his attempt at being a nice guy hadn't fooled

her. But either way, he wasn't sure his true aim had been for her to leave. "Where are you going to go?"

"Does it make any difference?" She took a deep breath and then frowned, as her hand slid to cup the underside of her swollen stomach. "Oh," she said. "Oh."

Mac's heart gave a jerk of panic. "What? Are you all right?" Oh, God, what if she was in labor? It was too early. Something was wrong. She could be in real trouble. "Does it hurt?"

She nodded and rubbed her stomach.

"I'll get you to a doctor," he said, deciding on a course of action and sweeping her off her feet and into his arms. "Who should I call? Do you have a doctor here? Nevermind, I'll take you to Dr. Graham. He's Hannah's doctor." He was all but running, his boots striking a heavy *clop-ka-clop* on the wooden dock, his arms cradling her protectively against him. "It'll be all right, Abbie. The baby will be all right. Don't worry."

"It's only a muscle cramp, Mac. What are you doing?"

He stopped dead, frowned down at the amusement glinting in her eyes. "A muscle cramp," he repeated dully. "You scared the living daylights out of me for a silly muscle cramp?"

"Well, it didn't feel silly on this end. It hurts like crazy for the few minutes it lasts."

"A muscle cramp," he said again. "You had a muscle cramp."

"Yes," she agreed. "But it's much better now, thanks."

There was laughter in her smile, a more relaxed look about her eyes, an appreciative warmth in the hand she had clasped around his forearm. Okay, so he was two for two in misunderstanding what she needed and attempting a rescue. ''Maybe I'll be a little less open-minded after this,'' he said.

''Somehow, I sort of doubt it.'' She looked at him and his heart, which was still racing from his scare, squeezed tight with the fierce longing to keep her near. ''You can put me down now,'' she said.

''Nah. I don't think so. No point in taking any chances on another one of those painful muscle cramps sneaking up on you.'' He shifted her a little more comfortably in his arms, bringing her closer to his chest. ''I'll just carry you all the way back to the house to be on the safe side.''

''I'm not going back to the house,'' she said, a shadow descending once again across her pretty blue eyes. ''They'll be calling for me there.''

''Who?'' Mac asked, but realized immediately who she meant. The gang. ''They're not going to call back. At least, not until you turn the phone on, and I'll just keep it in my pocket to make sure you don't do that.''

''You gave Brad your name. It won't have taken him five minutes to connect Mac Coleman with my friend Jessica Coleman, and from there, it's only a hop, skip and a jump to finding the Desert Rose ranch. Trust me, he'll have the house, the office, and probably the barn phone number before you can walk back up that hill and into the courtyard.''

''You don't have to talk to him, Abbie. Or any of the rest of them.''

She sighed, as if he couldn't possibly understand. "It's complicated, Mac, and it's easier if no one in the house can say for sure where I am."

"How did you ever get mixed up with a guy like that?"

Abbie shook her head. "It's the trying to get *un*-mixed up that has caused me all the problems. Put me down. I'll just stay out here for a while and hope no one decides to bring out the cordless phone."

Mac decided he was zero for two in the rescue department. Maybe the third time would be the charm. "No reason you should have to take any chances. I know the perfect place." Still holding her tightly against him, he headed off in the opposite direction. "No one will think to look for you there."

"Great," she said. "Now I'm being kidnapped."

"Give me some credit," he said, glad to hear the happier tone in her voice. "I'm doing my best to be a hero here."

Chapter Seven

The trouble with heroes is that they were men, Abbie decided as Mac set her feet on the floor in the dark front room of the guest house. It was perfectly clear to her that, since hijacking her phone and her conversation with Brad, Mac was determined to rescue her whether she needed rescuing or not. Sad to say—because she believed they all meant well—but her heroes just seemed to make things worse. She wished, just once, that the men in her life would allow her to save herself from disaster, instead of complicating most everything she tried to do. ''Thanks,'' she said. ''But this really isn't necessary.''

''It's no trouble at all,'' he said, misinterpreting her comment as gratitude. ''I think there are some candles around here somewhere.''

''Don't you have electricity out here?''

''Well, yes, but turning on the lights would be as good as sending up a flare. Someone would be over here within ten minutes to check on the place. Once they know you're out here, anyone might answer the phone in the house, transfer the phone call out here to the guest house and then, you'll be right back where you started.''

''I wouldn't have to answer the phone,'' she said logically.

''Then someone would have to come over to find out why the phone isn't working or why you didn't answer when it rang.''

''Sounds just like home.'' She looked around as her eyes grew accustomed to the dusky light. Across one long wall, curtains were drawn and Abbie felt her way around the furniture to reach them. When she found the cord and drew open the drapes, the floor-to-ceiling windows rewarded her with a beautiful view of the lake and the reflections of pinpoint stars and a silvery quarter moon in the dark water. ''This is nice,'' she said.

''Mmm,'' was Mac's reply, unless she counted the rummaging sounds coming from the far corner of the room. ''You sure you want the curtains open?'' he asked. ''Anyone passing close enough could see you standing there.''

Her lips curved, despite the fact that she had next to nothing to smile about. ''I'm not hiding out from the Mob,'' she told him. ''Only from my brothers and, luckily, they're not anywhere near this neighborhood.''

The rustling-in-the-drawer sounds stopped. ''Brothers?''

''Brothers,'' she answered clearly. ''Four of them. All big, burly and fiercely opinionated.''

''You're hiding out from your *brothers,*'' he repeated.

"That's right."

"Your brothers," he said again, as if he couldn't quite get his mind around the concept that she had brothers. "Not some abusive boyfriend and his gang?"

She laughed, wondering how he'd gotten such an idea. "Brad is my brother. He's second in the lineup of older brothers, right under Quinn, but ahead of Jaz and Tyler."

"Brad is your brother," Mac said, obviously still struggling with his previous misconception. "Why did you lie to your brothers?"

She sighed, still looking out the window at the night-dusted lake. "I knew the minute I told them the truth, my bid for independence was over."

"What truth? That you're on a ranch in Texas instead of at a camp in the Poconos?"

"That, and the news that in four months I'm going to make them all uncles."

She heard the scrape of a match and turned as Mac's frown came into view over the flame of a burning candle. "They don't know you're pregnant?"

"They didn't, but now that you've mentioned my *condition,* they've probably figured it out."

"Well, hell," he said succinctly.

"My sentiments, exactly."

"What about your parents?"

"I haven't told them, either," she admitted, ashamed of her delays. "At first, it was too embarrassing and then later, I felt I needed some time to think about what to say."

"How hard can it be to say, 'Mom, Dad, I'm pregnant'?"

"Plenty hard," she snapped, suddenly irritated. "Look what happened when I told you."

Silence fell like a net, dense and constricting, around her. She hadn't meant to bring up that sore subject. "There is a difference," he said finally, his voice as cool as an ice storm.

"Yes, *they* will believe me."

"I didn't doubt for a second that you were pregnant."

"No, only that you had anything to do with it."

He set the candle in its brass candlestick on the table, his movements methodical and calm. "Arguing with me isn't going to help your situation with them, Abbie. You have to tell them...the sooner the better."

"Gee, I wonder why I never thought of that." She wanted to be angry. With Mac. With every one of her brothers. With the staff at Miss Amelia's Academy. With the sun, the moon and the stars. But there was only herself to blame and she was getting really tired of being angry with Abbie. "Can we not talk about this? You've made it very clear you don't care what I do or where I go as long as I don't make any demands on you."

"That isn't exactly true, Abbie, and you know it. I've gone out of my way to be nice to you this week and..." His admission trailed away and she realized she'd been right to suspect his motives.

"What were you hoping to do, Mac? Trap me into admitting my devious designs on your checkbook? Trick me into thinking you'd had a change of heart?

Kill me with kindness so you'd have a clear conscience after I was gone?''

''I lost a wager with Cade,'' he said tightly. ''He advised me to give you a chance and when I balked, we drew straws. I lost.''

Her heart hurt, as if it had shriveled inside her chest. ''That's a relief. I'd hate to think you gave me a chance because you thought it was the right thing to do.''

''I have my reasons for doubting your story, Abbie.''

''What? Now you're going to tell me you're incapable of fathering children?''

''No, but I am not nearly so gullible as I was before.''

She frowned, confused. ''Before I told you about the baby?''

His eyes narrowed in the soft candlelight, then he walked past her and stood facing the windows and the lake beyond. ''A couple of years ago, I was in love with Gillian. She got pregnant and I proposed immediately, thinking that we'd just gotten a jump-start on the future we would have had together anyway. The wedding was planned, everything was perfect until the night of my bachelor party, when one of Gillian's oldest and closest friends got rip-roaring drunk and labeled me an A1 chump behind my back. The laughter and the whispers got louder until they finally got to me. Seems Gillian had known who I was a long while before she wrangled our *accidental* meeting. Seems, too, she'd been afraid I wouldn't propose to her without a certain push in that direction and since I proved cautious, she persuaded her *friend* to help her. It was his baby, not mine.''

Abbie was stunned. ''She confessed that to you?''

''No, all the evidence came secondhand. She maintained her innocence right to the end.''

''The end of what?''

The line of his lips was grim. ''Right up until the day of the wedding when Uncle Randy offered her a check to walk away then or take her chances in a divorce proceeding if the paternity test proved she'd been lying all along. She took the check and walked.''

''I'm sorry,'' Abbie said. ''That must have been awful for you.''

He turned to face her. ''I got over it.''

No, you didn't, Abbie thought. *You're just blaming me for someone else's lies.* But she didn't think this was the time to challenge him on that. Maybe, though, it was the perfect time for a dose of truth. ''I did not know who you were until we met at the airport, Mac. I was as shocked as you were. I didn't come here to trap you, trick you or humiliate you. I came because Jessica invited me and because I couldn't bear to go home and face my family's disappointment. And I don't really care whether you believe that or not.''

His eyes held hers, searching for a faith she didn't have the power to give him. ''So what happens now?'' he asked finally.

She shrugged, wondering why she'd expected—hoped—he would change his mind and accept her truth as fact. He was a son of royalty and of Texas, a prince, both arrogant and justly proud. Why had she thought for a second he would take a commoner like her at her word? "What happens is, we blow out the candles and walk back to the house," she said. "Tomorrow, I'll go home to Little Rock and you won't ever have to give me another thought."

"I don't think I'm going to stop thinking about you."

"Sure you will. It'll be easy. One pain-in-the-butt out of your life, just like that!" She tried to snap her fingers, attempted a smile but suddenly her eyes were awash in tears and she couldn't see. "Sorry," she said over a sudden lump in her throat. "Guess I'm just a little...blue tonight."

"Don't cry, Abbie." He moved toward her, and she turned away to hide her tears from him, but he put his hands on her shoulders and drew her back against his chest. "I don't want you to cry."

She hiccupped softly, blinking furiously to stem the tide. "I don't think you can stop me, Mac. Not even to win your bet."

He was very still for a moment, his hands massaging the muscles of her upper arms. Then, like a whisper, she felt his lips at her ear, the sensual distraction of his kiss in the hollows of her neck. Warm shivers raced in every direction—down her back, across her chest, to the tips of her breasts and the nape of her neck. Toes, fingertips, even her hair seemed to tingle with a heady anticipation. "Oh," she said on a long breath, "you shouldn't do that."

"I'm sure you're right," he murmured against her skin. "But I've run out of ideas on what else to do with you, Abbie. Making love to you seems to be the only alternative."

She gulped, wanting more than she wanted her next breath to believe he meant that. ''Mac, I...this isn't a good idea.''

He nuzzled from the hollows of her shoulder to the indentation below her ear. ''You'd rather cry?''

''No, but...''

''You're trembling, Abbie. Are you afraid of me?''

She ought to be. He had hurt her with his suspicions. Even if she stayed with him tonight, if they made love, it wouldn't change anything. He'd still believe the worst of her tomorrow. But oh, she wanted to stay, wanted to know the powerful passion in his kisses, his arms, his body. ''No, Mac,'' she whispered, leaning against him, giving herself permission to accept the support of his embrace. ''I'm not afraid of you. I probably should be, but I'm not.''

He mouthed the lobe of her ear to reward her bravery. Or perhaps only to drive her crazy with wanting. Desire pooled deep within her, overriding her sense of self-protection, persuading her that the only thing that mattered was what she was feeling now—his lips, his hands, the seductive, wet tip of his tongue as he trailed a kiss along the curve of her jaw, nearly to the corner of her mouth, then slowly retraced the path to her ear. ''That's good,'' he said, pulling aside the strands of her hair and wrapping its weight around his hand. ''Because I'm scared to death of you.''

''That's...nice.'' She didn't know if he meant it, didn't care. It was nice...no, more than that, it was wonderful beyond her imaginings to have him touch her again, to feel his kisses on her skin, to drift into a world of pleasurable sensations she had only found once before. ''So nice.''

He tugged on her hair, persuading her to tilt her head back and expose her throat to the stroking caress of his fingers. ''You're so beautiful, Abbie. I want to touch you everywhere, feel you all around me, make love to you from now until dawn, but...''

He was going to reject her, punish her for her perceived betrayal. He had brought her to surrender and now he would stop the kissing and caressing because he didn't want her at all, and she would die of wanting him. ''Please, Mac,'' she said. ''Make love to me. All night long.'' Like a flower to the sun, she turned her face to him and offered her lips as a sacrifice. Then she was kissing him and he was kissing her and their breaths mingled with a prescient knowing. His arms folded in around her, pulling her tightly, fiercely, against his hard, male body. Desire flared, turned to flame and licked through her veins at the speed of quicksilver. He swung her into his arms and carried her out of the candlelight's flickering circle and into the dusky darkness beyond it.

She didn't know where he was taking her, and didn't care. His mouth over hers, his arms under her, his scent surrounding her, his chest supporting her. That was all she needed. That and more. Anything he would give her, she would accept and be glad for. She'd thought she would never know this fever pitch of passion again, had thought fate had allotted her only one night out of a lifetime. Whatever this second night might eventually cost her, she would pay the price and not complain. Ever. For as long as she lived, she'd hold the memory close and know that having sex was not, never could be, the same as making love.

They must have reached a bedroom, because when he laid her down, she felt the cushion of a mattress beneath her. The room was darker than the other one, lacking the row of windows and the pearly glow of night, but she could make out the shadow of him and her hands reached to pull him down with her. He closed his hands around hers, pressing them between his own, denying her request as he sat on the edge of the bed beside her.

"Abbie?" Her name, soft and compelling, floated to her through the dusk.

"Here."

She sensed his smile even before she heard it in his voice. "That part I know. What I don't know is, can you do this?"

"Yes," she said. "I can."

Still holding her hands between his palms, he leaned in to kiss her lips, lightly, sweetly. "Abbie," he murmured, then again, "Abbie."

"Mac," she murmured back, thinking that might be the right answer, the one that would bring him, naked and hard, into her bed, into her body.

One hand came up to brush across her forehead, linger against her cheek. "In five months, I've never been able to figure out why I didn't insist on knowing your name. Abbie. Your name is one of the most intimate things another person can know about you, and yet, I didn't ask and you didn't tell me. We were intimate in every other way, except perhaps, one of the most important. I regret that, Abbie. Not just because I had no idea how to find you after, but because I wanted to caress you then with the sound of it, whisper it to you as I entered you, say your name over and over in the throes of ecstasy, and murmur it sweetly into the sated aftermath of our passion. Abbie…Abbie…Abbie.''

She shivered with the husky sounds, wanting so much more than she feared she could have. ''Mac…?'' She made his name a whispered question and moved to sit up and meet his kiss somewhere in between. But his hands urged her back to the pillow, held her without force. ''Please, Mac?''

He touched a fingertip to her lips, released her hands and placed his palm lightly against the hard round curvature of her pregnancy. ''I want to make love to you, Abbie. But you're pregnant and I don't know if you…''

Hope, that optimistic flower, blossomed and multiplied a thousand times over. ''Yes,'' she told him simply. ''I can. I really can.''

Again his smile came to her mind. ''Yes, but are you sure it's safe?''

She almost laughed aloud, giddy with anticipation. ''Well, I'm already pregnant, so we're safe on that score at least.''

''You know what I meant.''

Thankfully, gratefully, she did. ''Sex is perfectly safe as long as you don't expect me to hang from the chandelier.''

His chuckle was low, throaty and wonderful to hear. ''Well, I was hoping.'' He let the teasing fade and asked more seriously, ''You're sure there's no reason to avoid the intimacy?''

''Positive. The doctor told me...and no, I didn't ask. She just thought I should be aware that sex is okay, encouraged even, as long as it's comfortable.''

''And you're not hanging from the chandelier.''

She reached for him, feeling the muscles of his arms flex beneath her fingers. ''We don't need a chandelier,'' she told him. ''We're using candles.''

There was the sound of a boot hitting the floor and it was, without a doubt, the sweetest sound Abbie had ever heard.

''No candles, either,'' he said as he slid down to lie with her on the bed. ''I'm not anxious to set this place on fire.''

She sighed happily into his kiss. ''You couldn't prove that by me.''

Something inside Mac changed when she said that. Not the desire. No, that was like a fever in his veins. But until that moment he'd held back, operated on impulse, sure that he could stop before things went too far. He'd touched her first to keep her from crying. He'd kept touching her because it seemed to distract her. The plan had worked like a charm, too. Except that he was the one charmed, the one who lost himself in the role of protector, the one who needed her touch more than she ever could need his.

So here they were, about to turn one mistake into two, complicate an already complicated situation. But something had happened with Abbie's soft admission of a desire so hot it burned him just thinking about it. He wanted Abbie again, wanted her wanting him.

It was more than that, though. It was possibilities, opening like opportunity in his mind. Maybe Cade was right. Abbie wasn't Gillian. She wasn't here to trick him, only to love him, to be desirable and fascinatingly seductive in his arms. Okay, so maybe he wasn't entirely sure of her motives. Maybe he wasn't ready to jump in and be a father to her baby. Maybe he never would be, but somehow, his heart had decided they deserved a second chance. ''Abbie,'' he whispered, just to feel the shape and texture and taste of her name on his tongue.

''Here.'' Her arms slid around his neck and pulled him to her and it was the only place he ever wanted to be.

THE EXTENSION PHONE JANGLED like an alarm clock on the bedside chest. Mac rolled over, blinked at the glint of daylight peeking through the closed shutters. He was in the guest house with Abbie, and the sensual memories of the night before rippled through him with sweet remembrance. The phone rang again and he reached for the receiver, quickly, quietly, afraid the noise or the movement would wake her. But she slept on, unaware of his gaze caressing her, unaware that she held him mesmerized with just the bare curve of her shoulder and the tangled loops of honey-brown hair curling haphazardly across it. He felt a sudden, sharp longing to touch her, protect her and forever keep her safe from harm, and an equally strong impulse to jump out of the bed and run as far and as fast as he could.

''What?'' He'd pitched his voice low and turned

his head to direct the sound away from Abbie, but sleep still cloaked his throat and he had to clear it softly and repeat, "What?"

"Mac?" Jessie's whisper rushed across the line to him. "Is that you, Mac?"

"Yes."

"Thank heavens, you're there. Well, on second thought, you probably ought not to be there just now. Is Abbie with you?"

Jessie was overly excited, he thought. Now that she'd figured out where he and Abbie had disappeared to last night, she was probably imagining all kinds of romantic scenarios. He smiled, thinking that at least on some level, she'd be right. "What do you want, Jess?" he asked.

"I called to warn you," she answered, sounding hurried and harried. "You're about to have company." Her voice dropped to a whisper. "Brothers."

Great. Cade was going to pop in to ride him about the wager and the way that short straw had been the ticket to a love match once before. He'd have Alex in tow to double the teasing allotment. "You don't have to whisper, Jessie." He did, though. Abbie was beginning to stir beside him. "I'll head those two hayseeds off at the pass. Thanks for the warning." He hung up and turned to see Abbie's blue eyes blinking open. "Hi," he said softly.

She smiled in answer, slid a hand up the length of his arm, across his shoulder and chin until her fingertip touched his lips in a lover's greeting.

He couldn't help himself, he shifted his weight, slipped down in the sheets and bent over her, pressing a good-morning kiss to her eyelids, her nose, her chin, her lips. "Mmm," she murmured against his mouth. "Mmm."

"Exactly what I was thinking," he said, trailing kisses down the slope of her neck all the way to the valley between her breasts. "But that was Jessie on the phone. Cade and Alex are on their way over."

Abbie sighed her disappointment. "What do they want?"

"Who knows. Occasionally they lose all sense of decorum."

"Mmm," she said as his fingers teased her nipple. "Sounds like my brothers."

The words hung there for a moment, gathering like omens as her eyes suddenly widened and stared into his. *Thud, thud, thud.* The heavy knock was the only tip-off they got before the front door of the house slammed open and they heard the sound of boots on the floor and voices...deep, booming basses every one of them. "Abbie?" One of them called.

"Are you in here, Abigail?"

"Come out, come out, wherever you are," said another in singsong fashion.

Mac looked up to see his Levi's draped over a slat of the ceiling fan, Abbie's draped over another, both pair making lazy circles overhead. His underwear and socks adorned the brass bedpost on his side of the bed. Abbie's unmentionables were scattered, like signal flags, wherever he'd tossed them last night. It had been fun at the time to fling clothes left and right. They'd laughed and made jokes about hanging from the chandelier. It had been the kind of intimate teasing that would be funny to them, but Mac knew it probably wouldn't be very amusing to a quartet of humorless brothers.

"Oh, no," Abbie said under her breath, obviously reaching the same conclusion as Mac. Staying in bed, with a sheet for cover, seemed better than greeting callers in the buff.

There was a tap at the bedroom door. "Abbie? You decent?"

She gave a tiny groan and called out, "Brad? What are you doing here?"

"Abbie, it's about time we found you."

The doorknob was turning, the door already opening, before Abbie's voice croaked out frantically "Stop! Don't come in..."

But it was too late. Brad—if the Herculean man in the doorway was that particular Jones brother—had already glimpsed the scene.

"...here," Abbie concluded dismally as one...two...three more brothers stacked up behind the first. They were all similar in size—big—and shape—Mr. Universe contenders. The front guy had hair as black as the Desert Rose stallions, but the back three had hair the color of Abbie's, only shorter. Much shorter. If the bodies had been a little less muscled, the hair a little bit longer, the skin a couple of shades tanner, any one of these guys could have fit right into an episode of *Baywatch.* All four of them had eyes as blue as Abbie's, only theirs were decidedly not as pretty. They did seem to have clear vision, though, and had already put the worst possible interpretation on the situation. Mac couldn't really blame them. It looked bad, he knew.

What was he thinking? It *was* bad.

"Morning, gentlemen," he said, hoping they were. "You can find some coffee in the kitchen. Abbie and I need a few minutes together before we do any entertaining."

"Appears you've already had a good many minutes together," one of the middle brothers said.

"And it looks like they were pretty entertaining for somebody." The guy in back leaned into the room, his focus on the circulating denims. Mac wished he'd thought to lock the guest house door last night. But normally, on the Desert Rose, a door being left unlocked wouldn't have been a problem.

Brad's frown deepened to a glower and he cut straight to the chase. "Are you okay, Abbie?"

"I was until you four showed up," she said irritably. "I don't know why you thought you needed to come after me like a dadgum posse."

"If we were a posse, we'd lose our badges for getting here after the horse is already out of the barn."

Lovely analogy, Mac thought, but Abbie seemed too agitated to care. "Well, you can just turn around and go back home."

The lighter-haired brothers shifted positions and Brad stepped on into the room, followed by two more, leaving one to fill the doorway all by his lonesome. "Introduce us to your...him," he said.

Abbie looked at Mac, an apology burning clearly in her eyes. "Mac Coleman," she complied. "These are my brothers. Brad..." She indicated each with a nod. ''Tyler, Jaz, and that's Quinn by the door.'' Her gaze turned back to the Jones men. ''Now you can go. I'll see you at home in a few days.''

Quinn crossed his arms at his chest, as if he could stay in that doorway for decades. ''We're not leaving without you and we're sure not leaving until we find out what *condition* you're in.''

Abbie's confidence took a nosedive. Mac could tell that in a glance. He slipped a hand beneath the covers, found hers, felt her fingers tremble and gave them a squeeze of encouragement. ''I'm going to ask you *gentlemen*—'' he stressed the word to make his point ''—one more time to wait in the other room. You're making Abbie very uncomfortable, besides which you're beginning to get on my nerves.''

Quinn looked surprised but not particularly impressed. ''First, we want to know what's wrong with our sister.''

''Nothing's wrong with me,'' Abbie said. ''I'm pregnant, that's all.''

Silence crashed into the room like a glass jar and shattered into a variety of shocked expressions. Under different circumstances, Mac might have laughed at the looks on their respective faces. But the circumstances were awkward, and he didn't feel a bit like laughing.

''What did you say?'' Jaz, the tallest of the crew, stared at Abbie.

''You're having a baby?'' Tyler, too, stared at his sister.

But Brad and Quinn turned identical glares on Mac.

"You?" One of them voiced the question of paternity, but clearly it was a joint project.

"No," Mac answered. "I'm not having a baby. She's the only expectant mother in the room."

Brad took a step forward, his fists clenched and ready. "All right, wise guy. The next words out of your mouth had better be the ones about how happy you are to be getting us as your brothers-in-law."

"Brad!" Abbie said, outrage quivering in her voice. "Get out of here. Now. All of you." Then she added an impassioned, "Please!"

"Not until we see the ring on your finger."

"Out!" She shouted and still they didn't move, just stood there eyeing Mac, oblivious to the pain and embarrassment they were causing their sister.

"We're not engaged, if that's what you're thinking." Mac was ready to evict these overgrown adolescents himself, in the nude, if necessary, to get them out of this room and give Abbie time to pull herself together. "That's a little old-fashioned, even for Texas."

"We don't live in Texas," Jaz informed him.

Quinn straightened in the doorway and his gaze shifted to Abbie. "Is he the baby's father, Abbie?"

Mac felt his chest tighten, knowing even before he glanced over at her bent head, her tucked chin, her lowered gaze, her defeated demeanor, exactly what she was going to say.

"Yes." The word was soft as a vapor, but it slugged Mac square in the heart. Last night he'd allowed himself to believe in her, believe in the possibility of a future with her, believe in love at first...and second...sight. And it had all been a setup. Beautifully done. Artfully executed, right down to the outraged expectation on the faces of her brothers. They could be in on it. Or they could have been manipulated as neatly as he had been. The only detail she'd failed to provide was the loaded shotguns so this could be a true shotgun proposal.

Four pairs of determined blue eyes turned on him. Four sets of slugger-sized hands folded into resolute fists. Four men stood shoulder to shoulder in their joint decision that Mac would marry Abbie. He was outnumbered, outflanked and—at least at the moment—out of options. So with as much dignity as he could stomach, he turned to Abbie. ''Will you marry me, Abigail Jones?'' he asked without a modicum of emotion or enthusiasm.

She lifted her head, looked straight into his eyes and said, ''No.''

Chapter Eight

It was always the same whenever her brothers were around. No one listened to Abbie. She could sneeze and instantly four handkerchiefs were hers for the duration. She could voice her appreciation for the rich tones of Andrea Bocelli and within days, she'd have the entire library of his CDs. She could casually mention that she was thinking about refinishing an old chest of drawers, and before she could give it another thought, her troupe of commando brothers had it ready for her to admire. She could wonder aloud the best way to avoid a construction zone and wind up with a detailed map on the quickest, most economical, safest and best way to get where she was going. But when she declared forcefully that she would not marry Mac Coleman, not a soul was listening. Anyone would think she'd blushed pink with pleasure and stammered out a delighted acceptance.

It had taken roughly five minutes after Mac's forced proposal and her flat refusal of it to get her brothers out of the bedroom. First there had been a scant two seconds of silence as her no bounced off brother after brother after brother after brother. Then

Ty grinned as if she'd made a very clever joke and said, "Don't mind her, Mac. She's just ticked that we were all in here to hear the proposal."

"She's always tried to be such an independent little thing," Jaz added.

"Don't worry, she'll marry you," Brad said.

"We're staying until after the wedding," was Quinn's thinly veiled threat.

Mac folded his arms across his chest. "I didn't doubt it for a second."

Abbie didn't know where to turn her argument and lost the opportunity as first one brother and then the other three moved forward to offer Mac a growl of insincere congratulations. She suspected each of the grudging handshakes they delivered were just this side of bone-crushing and contained more warning than welcome-to-the-family. Certainly, not one of them—including Mac—smiled at any point in the proceedings. Oh, no, the smiles—excluding Mac's—came as each of her brothers skirted the bed to deliver a proprietary and very big-brotherly kiss on her cheek.

"Don't worry about a thing," Quinn advised her.

"You okay now?" asked Jaz, who—no surprise—didn't wait for an answer.

"You'll be a beautiful bride," Tyler assured her.

"We'll take care of everything," Brad said.

She managed to keep the covers pulled up to her neck and refrained from screaming at them to get out. Not that screaming was apt to have any more favorable effect than not screaming. They weren't going to listen to her either way.

So she held her tongue and her temper in check,

suffered silently with a fast-shifting array of high emotions—anger, embarrassment, exasperation, frustration, and indignity, to name a few—and waited for the Jones men to get out of the bedroom. But her brothers were in no hurry to leave her alone with Mac and would probably have escorted her out of the bedroom if she'd been wearing even a stitch of clothing. As it was they seemed to be debating their exit, asking and answering each other's questions, discussing how soon the wedding could take place, where and what time of day, what kind of reception they ought to plan. The four-sided conversation turned to which one of them should call Mom and Dad, who were preparing for a long-planned anniversary trip to Hawaii. The wedding, Brad and Quinn had decided, should take place before Bill and Edie flew off to Maui, which meant it had to take place sooner rather than later. Considering Abbie's condition, however, any wedding was already later than it ought to have been.

But finally the brothers tromped out of the room, saying they'd bring in some decaf coffee for her the minute it was ready, advising her—with a final shot to Mac—that they'd be right outside the door should she need them. She released a long, heartfelt sigh the minute the door closed behind them and realized, suddenly, she was angrier with Mac than with any one of her brothers. They, at least, had her best interests at heart, however misguided their methods. Mac on the other hand…

She turned to him, ready…eager, even…to vent

her frustrations. "I don't know what you thought you were doing, proposing marriage like that."

He threw back the covers and hauled his butt out of bed, giving her a premium view of his backside, but otherwise ignoring her, which made her even madder.

"You should have let me handle them," she said.

He raised one arm, reclaimed his Levi's from the ceiling fan with an efficient little jerk and pulled them on in precise, tightly controlled movements. "I'd say you've handled this perfectly already. You should quit while you're ahead."

He thought she'd planned this. After last night, he still thought she was lying. "You're the one who told them where to find me," she said tightly in her own defense.

"I'm sure you had an alternate plan to get them here. I just jumped in to play the hero and saved you the trouble." He pulled on his boots with such force she thought he might shove his foot right on through the sole. "Either way, you're getting what you came for, aren't you?"

She wished she had one of the boots to throw at him. "I don't want to marry you!"

He stood, grabbed his shirt and headed for the door. "Yeah. If I were you, I'd stick to that story. Adds a nice touch of maidenly outrage to a premiere performance." Then he walked out and closed the door quietly but decisively behind him.

Abbie hadn't wasted any time after that attempting to educate her brothers about the mistake they'd made. She hadn't even bothered to try to correct their erroneous assumption that she would marry Mac because they believed that she should. Instead, she answered a few of their questions about her job and dismissal from Miss Amelia's Academy, and she did her best to persuade them that no amount of interference on their part would get her reinstated. She ignored their inquiries into where, when and how she'd met Mac, admitting only that she had met him the night of the graduation party. In answer to why she'd picked Texas, of all places, to hide out in, she'd said simply that her friend, Jessica, had invited her. It wasn't until Quinn wanted to know what in heck had prompted her to invent a summer camp in the Poconos instead of coming straight home to tell her family she was in trouble, that she clammed up like an oyster and said she wasn't really feeling well enough to talk about it.

Perhaps because her *condition* was apparent and unavoidable, now that she was up and dressed in her maternity jeans and big shirt, not one of them seemed eager to mention it. Abbie figured they'd pretend it wasn't the reason they were set on getting her married and had decided amongst themselves not to say anything at all about the baby until after the wedding had made an honest woman of her again. Which would be just fine with her. She didn't want to talk about the baby yet. She hated knowing that she'd disappointed them, but regret wouldn't undo even one of the mistakes she'd made. Better all around to spend her energy on not making the further mistake of getting married for all the wrong reasons.

An hour later, she'd escaped to the big house,

showered, changed her clothes and found refuge in the office. She settled behind her desk to brood over the mess she was in now while Jessica argued loudly and apparently without much success with Nick Grayson, the son and heir of the Dallas branch of Coleman-Grayson. Abbie didn't actually know that was who was on the other end of the phone conversation, but since Nick seemed to be able to incite Jessie's red-haired temper simply by being on the same planet, it was a good guess.

A few minutes later, Jessie slammed down the phone and glared at it for good measure. "Eat dirt and die, Nick Grayson!" she said, confirming Abbie's suspicion. "That man is so stuck on himself he probably saves the stubble from his razor for future generations to marvel over. Yuck! I know Dad has always wanted me to take over the management here, but I swear, Abbie, if I have to work with Nick, I'm not sure I want to learn to run this damn company!"

Abbie offered a sympathetic nod, although privately she thought she'd happily trade all the obnoxious men in her life for the one who was a bee in Jessie's bonnet. Nick had been very nice to her the couple of times they'd spoken over the phone. "My brothers are here," she said to Jess, getting straight to the subject she knew her friend was dying to discuss. "Still want that introduction? Take your pick. There's four of them and I'll give you a discount if you take more than one."

Jessie's cheeks stayed flushed in the aftermath of her argument with Nick, but she did manage a wry smile. "I met them earlier. Four big, good-looking guys who hopped a red-eye flight to Austin because they were worried sick about their baby sister.''

''Yes, well, now they're just worried about getting her married.''

Jessie didn't seem surprised. ''I heard. They're going to be staying in the guest house until after the wedding,'' she said, which wasn't exactly news to Abbie, either. ''I'd say it was a wholesale Jones invasion, except that Mom invited them to make themselves at home. I guess your parents will be coming, too?''

Abbie sighed, dreading everything about the day ahead of her. ''I hope not. I told Quinn that I wanted to be the one to phone them today and explain what's happened. If my brothers will let me do that much, maybe I can stop Mom and Dad from making an unnecessary trip.''

''I, uh, wouldn't count on that,'' Jessie said, her expression sympathetic but consoling. ''I think my mom's already offered to call and invite them to stay here, too. Knowing her, she's probably already phoned, and double-checked whether they take their coffee black or with cream and sugar.''

Abbie appreciated the Colemans' generous hospitality. She really did. But she wished they didn't have to be such gracious and accommodating hosts. ''I'll straighten it all out somehow.''

''You want to practice on me?'' Jess suggested.

Abbie sighed, knowing she had to start somewhere and deciding she'd keep her account brief and vague until she'd sorted out the rumors circulating among the Colemans. ''Mac proposed,'' she said dully.

Jessie's eyes widened in surprise. "He did?"

Oops. Obviously that detail hadn't made it into the loop.

"I thought maybe your brothers just sort of took that part for granted." Sinking into the desk chair, Jessie seemed momentarily lost for what to say. "But he actually said the words 'will you marry me?'"

No point in denying it now. "Yes."

"And what did you say?"

"No."

"No?"

Abbie frowned at her friend's astonished response. "Did you expect me to go along with this wedding nonsense just because my brothers are behaving like insane dictators?"

Jessie made a face. "No, I thought you were getting married because Mac said you were."

"Mac said that?" The last Abbie had seen of him, he'd been walking out the door, too furious with the world to offer a word of explanation.

"He walked into the kitchen over an hour ago and announced to everyone assembled there that he was the father of your baby and the two of you would be getting married right away. Then he walked out, leaving us in something of an uproar."

Abbie lifted her chin. "He said that?" Surely Jess was exaggerating, putting her own spin on what had actually been said. Mac wouldn't suddenly claim paternity of the baby he was dead set on denying was his. He might have said she was claiming the baby was his. He might have said she was insisting he was the father. He might even have said she didn't know who the father of her baby was. None of which made any of this easier. ''Who was there?''

''In the kitchen, you mean?'' Jessie thought back and ticked off the names. ''Me, Mom, Dad, Aunt Rose, Hannah and Alex, Ella and Hal, Stanley Fox, Olivia, and a couple of the boarders...Savannah, I think, and oh, I can't remember the other one's name right now.'' She turned a wry expression to Abbie. ''It was a good crowd. I imagine everyone on the ranch has heard about it by now.''

Abbie wished her bones would just dissolve so she could slink through the floorboards and slither off into oblivion. ''And I thought getting fired because I was pregnant was as embarrassing as it could get.''

''I guess getting caught in bed with Mac sort of upped the ante, though, huh?'' Jessie said, then added a sly, ''You were in bed with him, weren't you?''

There didn't seem any point in lying about that, either. ''Yes,'' she admitted glumly, and decided to just confess the rest of the story and get it over with. ''Mac is the mystery man I met at our graduation party. We spent that one night together, I left the next day for my job, but I swear, Jessie, I had no idea he was your cousin. I didn't know until I got here.''

''And he had no idea you were the friend I'd begged to come help me in the office.'' Jessie didn't wait for Abbie to confirm or deny it, as the pieces of the story began to fall into place for her. ''I wondered why he was so interested in who I'd been in school with, and why he kept asking questions about what my friends were doing since graduation, as if I'd know about every single person who made an appearance at that graduation party. I can't believe he was charming enough to sweep you off your feet and then was too backward to get your name. He must have been really intoxicated.''

''He wasn't drunk,'' she said, offended. ''And neither was I. It was just the atmosphere.''

''I didn't mean to make it sound like he'd have had to be drinking to fall head over heels for you in the space of one night, Abbie. I'm just surprised that after being so cautious for so long he'd fall hard without being absolutely certain of who you were.''

''That was my fault. I wanted to be anonymous, mysterious. I had plans, you know, and didn't want the complications.'' Abbie sighed. ''Boy, was that a stupid idea. The Fates were probably lined up, jostling each other to be first to hand out my comeuppance for that bit of impertinence.''

''I knew something was going on the minute the two of you walked in after he picked you up at the airport, but it didn't dawn on me that he was the baby's father until a few days later when you and I were talking. You could have told me, Abbie. I am your friend.''

''But he's family.''

''One doesn't cancel out the other. It makes you just that much more special to me.''

Surprise brought a sting of tears to her eyes, but Abbie blinked them back. She wasn't crying—or even coming close to it—today. Too much depended on her getting this situation straightened out. Hormones or no hormones. ''You believe me?'' she asked simply.

Jessie's quick frown was reassurance in and of itself. ''Why wouldn't I?'' Then, in an instant, the frown switched to a look of comprehension. ''Mac doesn't believe you, does he? He thinks you set him up, got pregnant on purpose, showed up here knowing he was a newly discovered prince. That's why he's been so angry lately.''

Abbie sighed. ''He doesn't believe it's his baby, either.''

''Since he asked you to marry him, Abbie, he must think that, at least, is possible.''

Abbie shook her head. ''I don't know why he didn't just tell my brothers to get the hell out of his bedroom and off his ranch. I don't know why he proposed. But I do know he's never going to believe I'm telling the truth about any of this.''

''A paternity test will convince him.''

''I'll die a slow and lingering death before I ever give him the satisfaction of submitting my child to that. He either takes us on faith or not at all.'' She paused, realizing what she'd said. ''Not that I care one way or the other what he does. If I'd known he would be here, I'd never have set foot on the Desert Rose ranch in the first place. No matter how much I wanted to see you.'

Jessie pressed her lips together, as if she had to stop herself from defending Mac further. She got up from her desk and walked around it, crossing the space between the two desks and reaching across the cluttered desktop to close her hands comfortingly over Abbie's. ''Don't worry. It'll all turn out for the best. He's going to marry you and make a home for you and the baby. After his experience with Gillian—I'll tell you all about her later—it's understandable he's a little uncomfortable with your brothers showing up and all. It's an awkward situation. But believe me, Mac would not have asked you to marry him if he hadn't been planning on doing it anyway."

Abbie shook her head, knowing Jessie would want to see her cousin in the best possible light. "He told me about Gillian," she said. "I know he's still bitter over the way she tricked him and you're right, it's understandable that he'd be leery of any pregnant woman who pointed an accusing finger at him. But I know for a fact, Jessie, he'd rather shoot himself through the heart than marry me."

It was clear from her expression that Jessie didn't believe that. She didn't, however, say so aloud, and for that and her friendship, Abbie was grateful.

"I think you could use some advice about how to handle a royal, princely pain in the butt." Jessie squeezed her hands in a gesture of support. "Come on. Let's go find Mom and Aunt Rose."

"I can't face them," Abbie protested. "They've been so kind and they're not going to believe me and...and my brothers are here, and it's all so awful."

"You're carrying Mac's child," Jessie said softly. "Trust me, the Coleman women are on your side."

"I SUGGESTED YOU TRY being nice to her, spend some quality time with her. I didn't advise you to sleep with her and then get caught by her brothers red-handed and bare-assed in bed with her." Cade stood next to his truck, one foot on the running board, one foot flat on the ground, preparing to head to Austin on business, but taking a few minutes to give his unsolicited opinion. ''Jeez, Mac, what were you thinking?''

''I wasn't,'' Mac snapped, angry with the world as a whole and his lot in particularly. He certainly wasn't in the mood to discuss the morning's events with his twin or anyone else. ''Just drop it, will you?''

''Well, I'd like to, but from what I've heard already, I don't think you can expect the subject to just up and go away.'' Cade tipped back the brim of his hat. ''Damn, Mac, Alex told me you stood right there in the kitchen and said straight out that it's your baby.''

''I also said I'm marrying her. Did he tell you that?''

''Yeah, he mentioned that, too.'' Cade gave his head a shake, clearly disgusted with the turn of events. ''It is your property, you know. You could have just ordered her brothers off it.''

''Not exactly the best way to start off with my future in-laws, now is it?''

''You're not going to marry her, Mac. I know it, Alex knows it, and you know it.''

''I am,'' Mac said, hating the conviction in his voice, hating Abbie for putting him in this damnable position, hating himself for being stupid enough to hand her the opportunity. ''And you can go to the bank on that.''

Cade looked completely bewildered. ''Why, Mac? Why not just laugh at the fools for thinking they can force you into a shotgun wedding? What can they do?

You're a Coleman. Hell, you're a damned prince! Why do you care what anyone else thinks?''

''You wouldn't understand,'' Mac said.

''Me?'' Cade took his foot off the running board and swung around to face Mac, hat back, jaw set, angry. ''It seems to me that it's you who's confused. A few days ago you were positive Abbie was lying about everything from when she got pregnant to the way she brushes her teeth. And suddenly today, she's having your baby and you're set on marrying her. What did she do to you last night to change your mind?'' Cade held up a hand, palm out. ''No, don't tell me. I don't want to know. But I do think you need to figure out why you're suddenly so ready to believe her.''

''I don't believe her,'' Mac said, knowing he couldn't explain even to his twin what had happened, knowing only that he'd rather marry Abbie believing she was a liar than to have her prove it by taking a settlement check as Gillian had done. ''But I'm marrying her anyway.''

Cade opened his mouth to say something else, then closed it abruptly. ''Fine. Then I'll stand up with you and be your best man. Just don't ask me to be happy about it.''

''That, at least, won't be a problem.'' Mac turned on his heel and walked away, feeling more alone than he'd ever felt in his life.

''HERE YOU ARE.'' Jessica sounded relieved as she pulled open the door leading to the courtyard and stepped outside, followed by a wan and hesitant Abbie.

Rose watched the two young women approach the bench where she sat with her sister-in-law. Vi looked up, too, as Jessie and Abbie came toward them, straightened and seemed to make an effort to compose herself. Rose patted her sister-in-law's shoulder supportively as she greeted the girls. "Hello there," she said. "Were you looking for us?"

"All over the house," Jessie said, stopping to fall in behind Abbie, who looked as if she might bolt at any second. "What are you two doing outside? It's nearly as hot as a chili pepper already."

"We were just looking for a quiet place to talk." Rose smiled, trying for a look that would indicate she and Vi had nothing better to discuss than a new recipe for dinner. "And it's not all that hot out here."

"It's getting there." Jessie lifted the weight of her own red-pepper hair off her neck and frowned at her mother. "Something wrong?"

So much for pretending this was just a casual chat between women who were sisters-in-law and friends. "Of course not," Rose said, adding a light laugh for good measure. "We were just talking, that's all."

"About me and…and Mac?" Abbie looked miserable and Rose's heart went out to her. She was so young to be pregnant and dealing with a personality as proud as Mac's. No matter what had happened between the two of them, Abbie shouldn't have to feel so responsible for what had, ultimately, been his choice as well as hers.

"No, not about you, Abbie," Vi stated with a sigh.

"We were talking about me and my next milestone birthday."

Jessica, being quite young herself, missed the point. "Oh, Mother. I wish you'd quit worrying about turning fifty." She turned to explain to Abbie. "I was born on Mom's twenty-fifth birthday and when I turn twenty-five in October, she's going to be fifty. Anyone would think she was going to be a hundred and fifty the way she keeps stewing about it."

"Jessica," Rose admonished softly, even as she wondered whether Randy had told his daughter about the party he was planning for their mutual birthday. It was Vi he really wanted to surprise. Vi, who needed the boost a party would give her. Unfortunately, it was also Vi who'd noticed Randy's interest in the beautiful boarder, Savannah, and jumped to the ridiculous conclusion he was thinking seriously about having an affair. Rose had sworn not to give away her brother's secret. She had promised faithfully not to reveal that Savannah was a party-planner and a part of the whole surprise, but this morning especially, it had been tough going to keep from telling Vi what was really in the works. She was actually glad the young women had interrupted them.

"Don't fuss at me, Aunt Rose," Jessie said. "You know she's worrying herself sick over gray hairs and saggy boobs and being older than dirt. Honestly, anyone would think she's going to wake up on her birthday and look so ancient she could pass for Father Time."

Vi straightened, her shoulders and chin rising simultaneously. "That would be Mother Millennium and fifty is not *old!*'' She turned to Rose with a renewed sparkle in her green eyes. ''Aren't you glad you only had sons, Rose?''

Jessie laughed, too confident in her parents' affections for each other and for her to be offended. ''She's probably not that happy about it this morning, Mom, considering Mac's announcement.''

Abbie gulped and Rose thought it advisable to offer her a means of escape, if she wanted one. ''You know, Abbie. I have some errands to run in Bridle. Why don't you come with me? We'll have lunch, get away from the ranch for a little while.''

''Thanks,'' Abbie said, looking guilty and grateful and desperate at the same time. ''That sounds lovely.''

''Great.'' Rose stood, dusting her hands, as if she'd been planning these errands for days now instead of minutes. ''I'll just get my things and meet you out front in—'' she glanced at her watch ''—five minutes?''

Abbie, still looking a bit shell-shocked, nodded and then, belatedly, turned to Jessie. ''I probably should finish those invoices today, though.''

Jessie rolled her eyes and gave Abbie a nudge. ''You've done more than your share in that office already this week. Go on. Have a good time. Barring a miracle, the work will still be there tomorrow.'' She sighed and turned to her mother. ''You are not going to believe what that stupid Nick Grayson has told me I have to do now!''

Rose slipped into the house, satisfied she'd done

her best to comfort Vi without ruining Randy's party plans. Now, she could, perhaps, help her second son by getting to know the young woman he'd chosen as his bride…and the mother of her first grandchild.

Chapter Nine

"Bridle isn't metropolitan, by anyone's standards," Abbie said after being seated at a window table in a cozy little restaurant called Nana's Home Cookin'. "But I think it's a perfectly charming old town. Thank you so much for letting me tag along while you did your shopping."

"I'm so glad you agreed to come along. It's nice to have the company." Across from her, Rose settled a floral napkin in her lap and smiled. "I believe Vi prefers shopping in Austin because of the selection, but I like the small-town atmosphere better. Even though, the first few times I came into town, people asked for my autograph, as if I were some sort of celebrity or something."

"Really?" Abbie was still a bit intimidated by this graceful, lovely woman who was Mac's mother. "What did you do when they asked?"

Rose laughed. "I signed whatever they handed me as if I were famous. My brother will tell you, I'm not shy."

"Well, you were a queen. I don't suppose many people in Bridle or in Texas, for that matter, can make that kind of claim.'' Abbie paused, wondering if maybe Rose was still a queen. ''I'm sorry,'' she said. ''I shouldn't have spoken in the past tense. You probably are still a queen, if you decided to return to your husband's country.''

''My country, too,'' Rose corrected softly. ''I still think of it as home. As to the other, although I was married to the king of Sorajhee, I could never think of myself as a queen. Of course, since Ibrahim's death, his brother, Azzam, has been king and his wife, Layla, is the queen. She was his first wife, which makes her also the chief wife in his harem and, by Sorajheean custom, the queen.''

''Harem?'' Abbie said, eyes widening. ''Were you the chief wife, too?''

''I was the *only* wife,'' Rose said, her expression stating clearly that there had been no other option. ''I would never have agreed to marry Ibrahim otherwise. Of course, at the time of our marriage, some Western ideology was filtering into the Arabic nations and, while the custom of having a harem is still accepted as a king's right, it's by no means expected or even necessarily encouraged. Still, a crown prince marrying an American heiress is not the norm and our wedding created something of a scandal at the time.''

''A scandal?'' This was better than the less dramatic account Jessica had given Abbie. ''You were the center of a scandal?''

Rose smiled. ''Not my choice for entertainment, I assure you. Ibrahim was the oldest son of King Habib Mohammed El Jeved and was promised to marry a young Sorajheean woman, but when he married me instead, there was an outcry to name Ibrahim's brother, Azzam, as the heir to King Habib's throne. It was a little frightening, but the king stood firm in his conviction that his oldest son should be crowned after his death and, eventually, the unrest died away." A shadow crossed her face. "At least it did for a while."

"So what happened to the young woman he was supposed to marry?" Abbie wanted to know.

"She was Layla, who married his brother."

"That must have made for some uncomfortable family gatherings."

Rose lifted her shoulder in a noncommittal and delicate shrug. "I sometimes thought Layla was jealous because Azzam took more wives and Ibrahim was fond of saying he could handle only one, when the one was the joy of his heart. I didn't have to share my husband with any other wives and there were times when I felt, perhaps, that she resented me for it. Other times, she was very proud of being a *proper* wife to Azzam, so maybe the traditional ways didn't bother her. It is still considered a great honor to be the chief wife. There is a great deal of power vested in the role." She smiled easily at Abbie as a dark-haired waitress approached. "Or so Layla has told me."

Abbie smiled in return, marveling at the courage it must have taken for even a sophisticated young woman—as Rose had obviously been at the time of her marriage—to choose to live in a country so different from the one of her birth. It could not have been easy, no matter how much she had loved her husband. Abbie ordered tea and a sandwich although she wasn't particularly hungry. Rose ordered a hamburger and a soda, confessing as the waitress walked away, "I haven't been back in the States long enough to get over my obsession with hamburgers. I wasn't all that fond of them before, but during my years in the sanitarium, it was the one food I honestly craved. In the course of many long days and longer nights, I promised myself that one day I would eat all the hamburgers I wanted. So far, I haven't reached my saturation point."

Abbie smiled, felt brave enough to say, "Jessie told me a little about your incarceration. She said they kept you drugged almost all the time. Why would anyone do that?"

Rose's expression barely changed, but it was enough for Abbie to know she hadn't fully forgiven those who had stolen years from her life. "I'm beginning to find out a few of the answers through my communications with Serena's father, King Zakariyya Al Farid of Balahar," she said. "He is a good man with many trusted advisors, and he continues to search for the truth to help me. Perhaps in time, I will be able to understand."

Abbie could tell that was all that would be said on the subject and had a feeling the conversation was about to turn to her. Much as she was beginning to like Rose, she really didn't want to confide in her. She was, after all, Mac's mother. Abbie gave voice to the first thought that flitted through her mind. "I don't think I could have done what you did," she said. "I couldn't live in a country where women are still often considered the property of men."

Rose raised an eyebrow. "I would have lived on the moon if that had been Ibrahim's home. But before I met him...? No, I never thought I could live in a country and culture so foreign to me. I certainly wouldn't have believed I would be happy there." Their drinks arrived and Rose tore the paper end from her straw and, raising it to her lips, blew the remaining paper covering clear across the room.

Abbie laughed, surprised by this childlike prank from the dignified and beautiful Rose. "I'll bet you didn't do that in Sorajhee," she said.

"Well, not at the formal dinners, anyway," Rose agreed with a laugh. "Ibrahim had a few things to say about my high spirits on occasion. I was as much a trial to him at times as he was for me. You should have heard some of the quarrels we had over my being a little too independent for a proper wife. Independence was always a touchy subject for me."

"It is for me, too," Abbie said, pleased to find this common bond. "Sometimes I feel I've been fighting to be independent my whole life."

"Your brothers?" Rose asked.

"Yes. My parents, too, to a certain extent, although I think they were just tired of trying to corral my brothers by the time I was born. Which, I guess, makes the boys sound like bullies and they're really not." She paused, wondering how best to describe her dear but exasperating family. "I suppose they're just so absolutely sure they know what's best for me."

Rose nodded. "It was the same with my husband.

He was so accustomed to never being challenged that I must have been a real shock to his system. With men such as your brothers and my sons, it always comes down to a matter of pride, I believe. They fear what they love will be stolen from them or that it will be lost through something they left undone. So their reaction is to control everything so it can't happen. Alex and Cade are learning now that real love is a balancing act. Mac is still fighting, but he will also learn to let go and trust in the power of love. Don't give up too soon on him, Abbie."

Abbie decided she had to be honest. "I'm not going to marry him, Rose. No matter what he said this morning."

Rose nodded and pushed her drink back as the food arrived and was placed in front of them. "I respect your decision, Abbie, whatever it ultimately will be. But for the sake of my grandchild and of my son, I pray that you will change your mind. I believe my son loves you, despite his fear." She looked at the hamburger on her plate and smiled like a kid with a sack full of Halloween candy. "I do so love hamburgers," she said, then glanced across the street. "After this, I need to stop at the post office and check for a letter I've been expecting. It's probably not there, but since I'm here I should find out, don't you think?" Her blue eyes looked wistful for a second, then she seemed to come back from a faraway place. "If you'd like to go to the little boutique and gift shop next door, Abbie, I can come back for you there when I've finished my business."

"That sounds great." Abbie thought it odd for

Rose, who'd only been in the vicinity a couple of months to have business at the post office. And a letter. The mail was delivered six days a week, excluding holidays, directly to the Desert Rose office. She'd sorted it several days, herself. On the other hand, Rose had lived a life Abbie could barely begin to imagine. How could she say what was odd and what wasn't for a woman who once upon a time had forsaken the only world she knew to marry a desert prince? "I'm so glad you invited me to lunch," she said instead. "Thank you."

"My pleasure," Rose answered. "It is definitely my pleasure."

ROSE ACCEPTED THE LETTER and the thick manila packet from the mail clerk. "Thank you," she said, and bestowed a grateful smile. "I've been so looking forward to receiving this. I didn't even dare hope it had already arrived."

"Got here this mornin'," the clerk said. "From—" he checked the customs form she'd signed in order to get the letters "—Ball-ee-har. Must be one of those countries nobody much has ever heard of."

"Balahar." She pronounced the name correctly but smiled to show she didn't mind that he hadn't recognized it. "It's near the Gulf of Oman and it's a very beautiful country, but you're right, unfortunately, not many people know much about it."

"You're that queen lady, aren't ya?" He asked, blushing to the roots of his sparse and receding hairline. "I figured it was you when I saw the postmark. "Royal Palace, Balahar.'"" He pronounced it correctly that time and she rewarded him with yet another smile. Really, now that the packet was here, she just couldn't seem to stop smiling.

"Thank you," she said again. "I can't tell you how glad I am to finally have these."

"Well, now, you're more'n welcome, ma'am. I'm happy to have been able to hold those for you until you could get in to pick 'em up. Course, that's my job, but I'm happy I could be of help."

"Yes," Rose agreed. "It was a great help. Not all mail is meant for all eyes, you know, and this—" she held the long, thick packet carefully in her hands, knowing its contents could be as precious to her as any gift she had ever before received "—this is very important to me. Thank you."

"Like I said, ma'am, it's my job."

Rose nodded and turned away. Even before she'd reached the door, she was cradling the package and letter against her body, protectively, as if someone might try to take this away from her. So much had been stolen from her already—Ibrahim, her sons, her brother, the baby born after she was taken to the sanitarium. So many things she could never reclaim. But now, perhaps, she held in her hands a gift she had had no hope of having.

Instead of going out the door, Rose changed direction and walked into an alcove of post office boxes. It wasn't as much privacy as she'd like, but it was presently empty and she couldn't wait any longer to read the letter Zak had sent along with pictures and newspaper clippings of his son, Prince Sharif. Well, at least, Rose believed the packet contained pictures.

Why else would Zak have sent a thick and bulky packet such as this? He could have said all he'd discovered in the letter. If Sharif was not her child by birth, then Zak could have had no reason to send a separate packet.

Drawing a deep breath, Rose opened the letter first and unfolded two sheets of stationery, all of which bore the imprint of the Royal Balahar seal and Zak's bold signature. She had become very familiar with his handwriting over the past couple of months and felt the increased rhythm of her heartbeat just at the sight of his name penned across the page. She and King Zak had much in common—Cade, Serena, a common interest in the future of the Sorajhee-Balahar alliance. And now, now perhaps, they would share a son as well. Sharif. His, by adoption. Hers, by birth. She smoothed the paper and read:

Queen Rose of Sorajhee and Texas,

Greetings from Balahar and the family of Al Farid. I trust my daughter and your son, Kadar, are in good health and happiness as I write this to you. I admit my heart is heavy with Serena's absence, but also light with knowledge that she is happy in her marriage. I hope to see them and you soon. Yes, Rose Coleman—El Jeved, I have discovered the truth and herewith, pass it to you. As you know, Abdul-Rahim, the trusted advisor of Azzam El Jeved discovered that Queen Layla paid the sanitarium for all the years of your confinement there. You were drugged to a state of irrationality, appeared at times lost to sanity and reason, and could not, therefore, be released. Layla was always obsessed with you, jealous because she was first promised to Ibrahim, before he married you. You stole Ibrahim from her. Or so she chants in the world of madness she has entered. Sadly, Azzam mourns her loss of reason, even as he accepts responsibility for your losses. He has aged many years in only months and, I believe, feels deep sorrow for all that has come to pass, especially the death of Ibrahim at Layla's direction, which he feels he might have prevented. He is a weak man and wanted the throne of Sorajhee more than he wanted truth. Now, however, he would welcome correspondence from you (he has told me this, himself) and would not protest a visit from his nephews, your sons.

However that may be, I know you await anxiously for the news we have discussed many times since you saw the picture of Sharif at Serena's and Kadar's wedding here. It is as you knew it to be. Sharif was brought to Nadirah and to me by your sister-in-law, Layla, as you already know. She told us then he was a foundling child, the son of her handmaiden, and as we were eager to have a son, we adopted him. Abdul has uncovered the evidence to support your belief Sharif was indeed the child you birthed after being confined in the sanitarium. Layla stole him away that same night and delivered him here to the palace in Balahar. It is a cruel irony that you were forced to mourn the child that was stolen

from you while Nadirah and I rejoiced in our great good fortune. Perhaps, however, you will come to believe that all works for good, and that my son, who is also the son of El Jeved, will one day be all you could have dreamed for him. Sharif is a good son, but headstrong and proud...like his fathers. I have not told him yet of his true heritage, but await your consult on the passing of this momentous information. As you will find, I have sent pictures of him as a child and as a young man, so that you may see him as you were denied during his growth years. It is also my hope to bring him to you in only a few weeks, so that you may know him as he is now. I confess, although I did not (would not?) see it before, he is very similar to Ibrahim as a young man. This, I feel, is what first brought him to your recognition. While I fear you must be weary of secrecy, I must ask that you share our plans to visit only with Serena, your brother, Randy, and perhaps, your other sons. The alliance is still fragile at times in our countries and I prefer to shroud the trip in secrecy for safety. It makes travel more tiresome, but seeing you again will soon refresh my spirit. I confess, with all modesty, that I hope you will look forward with pleasure to seeing me, as well as your fourth and last son, Sharif.
With all sincerity.

His signature completed the letter and, through a mist of tears, Rose thought it was the nicest, best signature she'd ever seen. Sharif was her son. He was coming to her. For the first time in her life, she would hold him in her arms. A fourth son. Ibrahim's son. Zak's son. She stroked the thick envelope that contained his pictures. Later, she would open the packet and see him as a child, as a young man. Zak was very kind to send them. He was, she thought, the kindest man she knew. Or perhaps, she was so happy today, any kindness would seem the best she'd ever known.

It was a glorious day and she placed the letter and unopened packet gently into the bag from Wilson's, the only department store in town. She'd bought a new blouse for Vi before she and Abbie had lunch, but now she wished she had bought gifts for everyone. She had received such a blessed gift, it seemed to her everyone should receive something special on this special day. A son. Over the past few months, she had received the precious gift of being reunited with her brother and his family, with Alim, Makin and Kadar, with a life she'd feared would never again be hers. But today…ah, today, she'd been given back the child she'd thought lost forever. Picking up the bag, Rose started for the door again, ready now to join Abbie in the Bridle Bright Boutique across the street. But once outside on the sidewalk, Rose stopped suddenly and laughed aloud. And then, she laughed aloud again. How many women, she wondered, learned on the very same day that they were about to become both a mother and a grandmother?

"…I'LL ONLY BE STAYING in the area another day or so." Abbie had fallen into conversation with the woman in the gift shop. She was a perky brunette, about the same age as Abbie, and had seemed eager to exchange a few words, no matter the topic. The gift shop wasn't busy on a weekday, she'd said. There wasn't a lot of traffic on the weekends at this time of year. The fall was better for business, or so she'd been told. Cooler temperatures was the reason. That, and more retirees passing through on their way to warmer climates for the winter. She didn't work at the gift shop once school started, though. She eventually introduced herself as Barbie Owens, a fifth grade teacher at Bridle Elementary School. Abbie said she was a teacher, too, only at the secondary level. Or rather, she had been. She wasn't returning to her former position in the fall.

"I can see you're trading the classroom for motherhood," Barbie said, her friendly Texas drawl as pleasant a distraction as the gift items on the store shelves. "When's the baby due?"

"September," Abbie said, and felt a jolt as she realized how quickly the time was passing. "Too soon, really. I haven't even begun to get things ready."

"I expect the baby will arrive whether you've gotten things ready or not. I sort of feel the same way about school starting again. The kids will come that first day whether I have the bulletin boards decorated or not." She laughed. "I guess that's really not the same thing at all, is it? I don't have any children yet. Haven't even been anywhere to meet my Prince Charming. One of these days, though, I'll get out of this two-horse town and see a bit of the world. I'll probably miss my fifth-graders, though. I love being a teacher.''

''I liked it, too,'' Abbie said, picking up a stuffed bear that was all fluffy and soft and a patchwork of pastel colors. She didn't have much money, but maybe it was time to spend what she had on a gift for the baby. The bear somehow made it seem almost real to her that in a little over four months she would be holding her baby in her arms. A single mom. Just her and her baby. And, of course, all of the baby's interfering, overbearing uncles. ''I'm hoping to find another position, though,'' she continued as if her thoughts hadn't strayed elsewhere. ''Maybe at semester.''

''I'll bet they'd hire you in a heartbeat up at the high school. Teachers don't stay long in Bridle because they can make better money in Austin.''

Abbie looked up, met Barbie's friendly brown eyes. ''I'm not staying in Bridle,'' she said. ''But thanks.''

Barbie shrugged. ''It was just a thought, and it probably wouldn't have worked out anyway. You'll want to stay home with your baby at least for the first year. People say that's the most important year, since they grow so fast and learn so much.'' The bell over the front door jangled as someone entered and Barbie's eyes widened before she leaned over the counter to whisper to Abbie, ''That woman who just came in? She was married to a sheikh. That's like a king over in Saudi Arabia, or some country near there.''

Abbie nodded, started to offer to introduce her to Rose, but Barbie leaned to one side of the counter to make sure her excited whisper couldn't be overheard.

"It was all over the news a few months ago that she escaped from a sanitarium in France and came over here to live with her sons. They're just down the road at the Desert Rose ranch. You should drive by there before you have to leave the area, see if you can spot one of the Texas sheikhs. That's what we call them here. Handsome." Barbie sighed dramatically and whistled under her breath. "Lord, they are fine. But we're not just talking handsome, either. I've heard they have real charisma, too. I'm dying to meet one of them."

Abbie didn't want to burst Barbie's illusions, but it seemed dishonest not to speak up. "Two of them are married," she said. "Happily, too, it appears."

Barbie sighed, long and low. "Figures," she said. "On the other hand, that means one is still available. I could get lucky, still yet."

Rose moved toward the counter and her smile seemed to light up the whole shop. "Isn't this a delightful place to spend an hour or so, Abbie? Do you love it as much as I do? We should buy something for the baby while we're here."

Barbie's gaze swung to Abbie, dropped to her waistline—or lack thereof—and swung back to Rose, who smiled and turned to look at a grouping of greeting cards before moving on down the aisle. "Let me guess," Barbie said in a tone clearly disappointed that Abbie hadn't given this information at the start. "You're married to one of the princes and expecting a little Texas sheikh of your own."

"No," Abbie answered, wishing for a return of the friendly spark in Barbie's eyes and smile. "I'm not."

"This," Rose said out of the blue. "We'll get this for the baby."

Abbie blinked as Rose returned, carrying a rocking horse, nearly half as big as she was. With a trill of laughter, she placed it on the counter in front of the younger women and stepped back to admire it. It was black, a squat, stuffed, furred fabric horse on rockers. Some clever store owner—familiar with the area's Arabian horse ranches—had made a costume of red and silver to turn the plain rocking horse into an Arabian. "See, Abbie?" Rose couldn't disguise her delight with the horse. "Someone's dressed it in Arabian show garb. Isn't that perfect?"

Abbie thought it was awfully large compared to the melon-sized shape of her stomach. But then in her mind's eye, she caught a glimpse of a dark-eyed, dark-haired toddler rocking back and forth and back and forth on the rocking horse. Her gaze fell on the price tag and she felt a jolt of amazement that a toy could cost so much. Her toddler, she decided, could learn to ride on a stick horse. "I'm not sure my baby needs a rocking horse," she said.

"Maybe not, but my first grandchild does. We'll take it," she said to Barbie who, probably realizing the size of the commission, recovered her bubbly voice just in time to say, "Will that be cash, check or charge?"

ABBIE AND ROSE STOOD SIDE BY SIDE at the back of the Jeep Cherokee, looking at the pile of shopping bags surrounding the Arabian rocking horse.

"We did some damage today, didn't we?" Rose said, sounding as delighted with her purchases now as when she'd started the spending spree. After the rocking horse decision, she'd concluded that she should get something for Hannah and her expected twins, too. There was only the one rocking horse, but Barbie was certain more could be specially ordered, so Rose specified the costume colors—each different so her grandchildren would know whose was whose. At the counter, she'd seen Barbie staple the receipts to the order forms with a see-through toy train and had to buy one of those for Jessie to use in the office.

After that, Rose was on a roll and had decided she should get a few practical items for the babies, as well. So back to Wilson's they had gone, where she bought a plethora of layette items, more than Abbie could ever imagine a dozen babies needing, much less only three. Then it was on to the other boutiques in town, to make sure they hadn't overlooked a hidden treasure along the way. About the time Abbie started to wonder if they'd need to rent a trailer to get everything back to the ranch, Rose returned to the Bridle Bright Boutique, where she'd insisted upon treating Barbie to an ice cream just because she'd been so helpful. Abbie had savored her single scoop of vanilla, held the patchwork bear—her only purchase—and hoped someday her child would know that at least one person had celebrated the news that a grandchild was coming.

But as they stood, looking into the gift-laden Jeep, Mac came out of the house and the pleasant aura of the day vanished. He had a ready smile for his mother, but it faded quickly when he realized Abbie was standing beside her. ''Been shopping, I see,'' he said, following their gazes. ''What is that?''

''An Arabian rocking horse for my first grandchild. Isn't it terrific?''

Mac growled something, Abbie wasn't sure what.

''I knew you'd like it.'' Rose patted his arm. ''Carry it into the house for Abbie, would you, please?''

His glance cut to Abbie, angry still and unforgiving, but he began taking shopping bags out of the car and placing them on the ground at his feet, until he could lift the rocker out. ''It's heavy,'' he said.

''That's so the baby won't tip it over,'' Rose told him pleasantly. ''Take it into the family room so everyone can see it, then later, you can move it up to Abbie's room.''

''Abbie doesn't have a room here anymore.''

Her heart gave a jerk. Had he thrown out her things? Packed them so she would have to leave right away?

''What?'' Rose said before Abbie could ask. ''Whose bright idea was that?''

''You'll need to ask her brothers,'' Mac said, backing up with the rocking horse in his arms. ''They moved her things out to the guest house, lock, stock and barrel this afternoon.''

Abbie was glad—for some stupid reason—that it hadn't been Mac. ''I wished they'd asked me if I wanted to move out there,'' she said, although that was like wishing they'd mind their own business. ''Where are they now?'' she asked with a sigh.

''Couldn't tell you,'' Mac replied as he headed for the front door. ''They seem to have been keeping tabs on my whereabouts all day, but I haven't been inclined to do the same for them.''

They'd been stalking Mac, like a bunch of two-bit detectives. Abbie was mortified. She would send them packing the minute she saw them. She would. ''I'm sorry they bothered you,'' she said, grabbing a couple of the shopping bags and following him toward the house. ''I'll talk to them.''

He stepped back, waiting for her or someone else, to open the door for him and the rocking horse. ''You do what you please, Abbie. I'm planning to stay as far away from anyone named Jones as long as possible. At least until the wedding. After that...well, we'll see how it goes.''

''This Jones will be gone before that. I'm leaving just as soon as I can make arrangements.''

''Probably shouldn't say things like that when there's a witness present.'' He indicated his mother, who was still getting packages out of the car, with a coolly indifferent nod. ''Be harder to save face later.''

''I'm not concerned with saving face,'' she snapped, irritated by his attitude, his tone of voice, just the fact that he was standing there holding a rocking horse that, until this moment, had been a cause for joy instead of rancor.

''If you say so.'' He shifted the toy in his arms. ''Could you get the door?'' he asked. ''This is beginning to get uncomfortable.''

She wanted to borrow Jessie's phraseology and tell

him to "eat dirt, and die," but instead she reached for the doorknob and said nothing at all.

He, on the other hand, didn't have the sense to quit while he was ahead. "I know this will come as no surprise to you, but the wedding plans have been pushed along very efficiently while you were out—" he glanced pointedly at the bags she held "—spending my mother's money."

"Makin," Rose said, coming quietly up behind them, two shopping bags in each hand. "Abbie was kind enough to allow me the pleasure of buying a few gifts for my grandchild."

"Oh, I'm sure she was delighted to give you that pleasure, Mother." He raised a wickedly dark eyebrow and, either because she recognized the don't-go-there message in his expression or because she didn't want to further embarrass Abbie, Rose said nothing more. She just took her purchases inside, followed by Mac with the rocking horse.

Abbie thought about turning on her heel right then and there, and walking away. Off the ranch. Out of Texas. But it galled her to think about giving Mac that much satisfaction, so she followed him into the house, resolved to keep a stiff upper lip, no matter what he said or did to make her uncomfortable. But inside the big house, she was greeted like one of the family, fussed over and included in Rose's enthusiastic recounting of their big shopping trip to Bridle. All the women and a few of the guys gathered round to admire the rocking horse and tease Rose about becoming a grandmother, and she didn't seem to mind in the least. Her happiness was contagious and Abbie's spirits responded with a decided lift. At least until she happened to look up and catch a glimpse of Mac's expression and the regret so evident in his dark eyes.

Her presence here in the midst of his family had cost him something more than self-respect, she realized. They had taken her in because he had declared that they should. He could more easily have branded her a liar and her child an interloper. He could have stood firm and his family would have stood with him against her. But instead, however reluctantly and whatever his motives, he had claimed responsibility, given her child the right to be born a Coleman, to share at birth in this large, extended and loving family. And now she was encircled in their acceptance, and he was on the outside.

Her heart faltered with the insight, not knowing if it meant there was room for hope or if it meant there was no hope, at all. All of a sudden, her resolve to nab her brothers and leave the ranch worked itself into a tug-of-war. She shouldn't stay, couldn't stay, but as Rose held up tiny little sleepers and passed around blankets as soft as a cloud, Abbie realized she had waited too late, already. Whatever Mac had meant to accomplish, whether he'd seen his announcement this morning as a stopgap solution or a slow and painful way to exact revenge, he had only added a new and deeper wrinkle.

Because now Abbie understood what she wanted.

And what she could never have.

Chapter Ten

Dinner that night was a big, boisterous gathering. The Jones brothers were far from antisocial. They enjoyed the food, the amiable company, the novelty of being houseguests, and were at their entertaining best to return the hospitality. And their best was very good. Abbie didn't know about other families, but her brothers could be wonderfully charming when they weren't trying to run her life. Despite being frustrated and out of patience with all four of them, she found herself laughing with everyone else at their "keeping up with the Joneses" stories. There had been hundreds of times over the years when she was genuinely proud to call them her big brothers and this was one of those times. Or rather, it would have been, if only the circumstances surrounding their visit hadn't been so embarrassing.

Across the table and down from her, Mac sat solemn and somber, with Cade on one side of him and Hannah on the other. Abbie was flanked by Brad and Jaz. No one else seemed to find it odd that talk of the wedding floated back and forth and up and down, exciting enthusiastic conversation all along the way, while the prospective bride and bridegroom sat a table-width apart, mostly silent, and heavily chaperoned. Mac didn't look at Abbie and the few smiles he handed out never came near her, but no one else appeared to notice that, either. She and Mac might as well have been invisible for all the attention they received. It was as if the planning had taken on a life of its own, and the wedding had become a thing apart from its two main participants or any basis in reality.

While she and Rose had been shopping, her brothers had enlisted the aid of Vi, Jessica, Ella, Hannah and Serena in finding a church, a minister, an organist, a florist, a caterer, and someone who—according to Ella and Vi—made absolutely gorgeous wedding cakes. The brothers had talked Randy around until he believed the idea for a combination wedding reception and Texas-style barbeque was all his own. The food was decided. The time, the place already set in stone. There were a few details, it seemed, still under debate. What Abbie would wear, for one. Whether Hannah, Serena, and Jessica—the chosen bridesmaids—would wear pink or blue. Music for the reception was still up in the air, although Stanley Fox knew someone who was a deejay on the side and would find out if he was available a week from Saturday. Abbie alternated between wanting to scream out her frustration and shaking her head in awe at her brothers' supreme arrogance and efficiency in doing it all without once asking her opinion.

Still, other than climbing up on the table and yelling out that she wasn't getting married no matter who was making the wedding cake, Abbie didn't see a lot she could do about it. Well, there was one thing. She could talk to Mac, find out what kind of cat-and-mouse game he was playing with her.

On second thought, she didn't want to know. What difference did it make in the long run, anyway? This whole unsettling wedding business was growing like Jack's beanstalk and, unless someone put a stop to it, she and Mac were going to wake up a week from Sunday and find themselves married. Wouldn't that just serve him right, too? But unfortunately, it would mean a loveless marriage, a marriage for all the wrong reasons and none of the right ones. Abbie didn't want that; neither, she was certain, did Mac. So they had to talk, had to decide the best way to stop this wedding nonsense. Whether he wanted to believe it or not, Mac had helped set this runaway train in motion and he was just going to have to give her a hand in putting on the brakes.

Getting a few minutes alone could prove tricky, though. Her brothers hadn't even begun to stretch their big-brotherly muscles yet. They had done a bit of pairing off, were showing signs that they wouldn't take lightly the task of watching out for their baby sister's interests. And her interests were whatever they decided they were and the course of action they had deemed best. The memory of her first high school prom date flitted like flypaper through her thoughts and stuck fast. She'd been sixteen. Her date had already turned eighteen. They'd had plenty of chaperons at the dance. But that hadn't stopped her brothers from showing up like clockwork every half hour, just to insure she was okay.

She was older now. So were they. But she knew from experience that very little had changed. At least from their perspective. They'd already moved her out to the guest house, and she felt certain that one or another of them would have a ready excuse to be on their way to anywhere she needed or wanted to go. They'd be nice. They'd be congenial. But they'd be with her twenty-four seven until after the wedding. Maybe even for days or weeks afterward. In their minds, Mac had had the pleasure of her company and now he would do the right thing by her and her baby, whether he wanted to or not.

Which only meant she and Mac would have to pull off some fancy footwork if they were to get more than five minutes of uninterrupted privacy. Abbie didn't know right off how it could be managed. Tonight was probably a bit soon to slip free of her brothers' surveillance. But it would happen. It had to happen. Because, one way or another, she and Mac had to talk.

MAC WAS AWARE of Abbie's surreptitious glances during dinner. He figured she was plotting something behind the unreadable expression in her blue eyes. Not that he let himself get caught watching her. He didn't want her to know he'd noticed the presumably new, particularly pretty, outfit she was wearing. Probably bought with his mother's approval and checkbook. He didn't want her to know he'd noticed how pale she looked, or how weary her smile. He didn't want to feel a pang of remorse for being less than kind to her both this morning and this afternoon. Hell, he didn't even want to be in the same room with her and all this jolly, jarring talk about weddings.

A wedding.

His wedding.

But it was too late now to reconsider. He'd laid claim to Abbie and her baby. He couldn't very well stand up in the midst of all the excitement and say he'd changed his mind, had decided Abbie was a liar and a cheat and probably wouldn't be able to pick her baby's real father out of a lineup.

Cade said something and Mac responded with a vague nod, pretending to be present in this moment he wouldn't remember a moment from now. He was weary, too. Seeing Abbie's brothers march into the bedroom this morning, like Sherman's troops into Atlanta, had crushed something inside him, left him too angry with himself to think clearly, made him wonder why he'd allowed himself to trust another woman with his heart. After Gillian, he'd sworn never to do it again. But then along came Abbie, with her soft smiles, laughing eyes and fiery passions to test his resolve. Like a complete idiot, he'd fallen for her. Not once, but twice. It was the height of foolishness he knew, but last night, he'd thought that…

Never mind what he'd thought, what he'd allowed himself to hope. Her strategy was too good, her outrage at her brothers' sudden appearance a little too convincing to be anything less than a part of a master plan. She had played an ace, but instead of calling her bluff, he'd topped her bid by playing the joker.

Well, so be it. In the next few days, he expected she'd try to convince him she was against the marriage, didn't want it, wouldn't bow to her brothers' wishes, even though he was convinced a wedding had been and was her aim all along. If she held true to form, he figured Abbie would do her best to persuade him she was angry at her brother's interference but helpless to do anything about it. Maybe he'd listen to her, if only to see how far she'd go to insure he was waiting for her at the end of the church aisle on Saturday.

Maybe he'd be there waiting. Maybe he wouldn't. Maybe he was an idiot to harbor even the faint hope that she'd call off the wedding before it got to that point. He didn't want to be the one to do it, to humiliate her—and himself—in front of his family and hers. He wasn't sure in his heart of hearts that he would, or could, do it when the moment arrived.

What he did know was that he was the biggest fool in Texas to want to offer her even that one chance to redeem herself.

ABBIE COULDN'T BELIEVE it was so difficult to get five minutes alone with the man she was supposed to marry in five days.

No, four days.

No, three.

The hours slipped away in a round of planning and shopping and getting things ready and, whenever she dug in her heels in an effort to get off the merry-go-round, someone was there to pick her up by the elbows and propel her right back into the saddle. The baby stretched and kicked and added his or her protests to the seemingly endless stream of activities, the must-do-this and the have-to-do-thats. Who could have guessed a wedding that wasn't going to happen could take such a lot of energy? Or be accomplished with so little interaction of the prospective bride and groom?

But either by accident or design, and Abbie was inclined to believe it was all part of a master plan by her brothers, she couldn't get a moment alone with Mac to tell him they needed to talk. Whenever she was entering a room, he seemed to be on his way out. When she went looking for him, one or more of her brothers fell into step beside her. When she did find him, he was with one or more of his brothers and didn't appear to be in any hurry to leave their company for hers. He seemed to have nearly as much protection as she did.

There. She'd given the strange feeling a name. It was as if he needed protection from her, didn't want to be alone with her, didn't feel the need to talk about what to do next. That was crazy, of course. She knew he didn't want to marry her. And she definitely did not want to marry him. Not like this. Not for all the wrong reasons. Not because someone else felt it was the right thing to do. Not because neither one of them had a choice.

Somehow, some way, she had to talk to him. Alone. And it had to be soon, because time was running out.

MAC WAS BEGINNING TO THINK Abbie's brothers had missed their calling. The CIA could have used them as a crackerjack surveillance team. If it had been only the four Jones brothers, though, he probably could have escaped their net. He did have the home court advantage, after all. But it seemed everyone on the ranch was eager to offer felicitations and advice on his approaching nuptials.

He couldn't walk from the stallion barn to the outdoor arena without being accosted by someone or another who wanted to talk about the wedding. He couldn't get from the house to his truck without running into someone eager to wish him happy. Congratulations were poured over him like confetti and he was slapped on the back so many times he began to wonder if Somebody Up There wasn't trying to knock some sense into him. The worst part of the whole business, though, was discovering that while he really wanted to dislike Abbie's brothers, they made it next to impossible. They were big, brawny, boisterous men who believed him to have enjoyed the pleasure of their sister's company and now simply expected him to take responsibility for it.

In a strange way, Mac understood their perspective and respected them for it. If Abbie were his to protect, he would take it as a matter of pride to see that she got what she wanted or needed. The Jones brothers were no different. They wanted him to do right by their sister, and as long as he was willing to do that, they were eager to know more about him.

At the house, at the barn, on their way to or from the guest house, one or another of them seemed always to be on their way to wherever he was going. They didn't talk much about the wedding to him, certainly never mentioned the baby, but he found it somehow reassuring, not to mention interesting, that they did want to talk about Abbie. He heard stories about her at age five, stories about her as a toddler, stories about her awkward stages, and stories about her first date. He learned about her desire to be a teacher and the tremendous debate within the family when she declared she was going to the University of Texas to complete work for her graduate degree.

Mac found it downright amazing that she'd managed to turn out all right under the kind of supervision her family obviously considered normal. It would have been perfectly understandable if she were afraid of her own shadow, much less of making an independent decision. It was clear her brothers didn't think she was capable of making a right choice without their collective assistance.

Slowly, without even wanting to, Mac began to see Abbie in a new light. While he was still pretty well convinced that she was behind the wedding plans, he was feeling a bit resentful that her brothers took so many decisions away from her. They decided, Abbie protested, and they acted as if she'd agreed. Or would, once she'd had a chance to think it over. It wasn't fair she'd had to deal with their control issues all her life. It wasn't fair her preferences couldn't be heard over what they absolutely believed was best for her. It wasn't fair that within days of their arrival, he'd gone from resenting Abbie's deceit to understanding a little of why she was so desperate to escape from her brothers. Marriage must seem preferable to continuing as she was, with her brothers hovering over her every move like overgrown mother hens. And marriage to him would guarantee that she no longer needed their consistent and persistent presence. Financially, Mac could provide for her and the baby in a manner that even her choosy brothers couldn't fault. How could they object if she married the man she claimed was the father of her baby, who also just happened to be rich and newly discovered royalty to boot? It would solve everything. At least, she undoubtedly thought it would.

And so, finally, it was her brothers' tireless vigilance over Abbie's every move that persuaded Mac to plot to kidnap her out from under their separate noses. He told himself she needed a respite from their watchful eyes. He told himself it was only right that he allow her the opportunity to do the right thing and call off her bloodhounds. He told himself the two of them needed to talk.

What he didn't say, what he barely allowed himself to acknowledge, was that he missed her and wanted to be alone with her. Regardless of the reason.

MAC HANDED JESSICA A NOTE. "Give this to Abbie."

She glanced at the folded piece of paper and handed it back. "Give it to her yourself. She's right over there," she said, indicating Abbie sitting not ten feet away on the sofa, squarely between brother Quinn and brother Brad. "In fact, you could actually talk to her. This is a free country, you know."

"It's not that easy to talk to her, in case you haven't noticed. She has bodyguards around the clock."

Jessie laughed. "And you expect me to believe you're afraid of them?"

"No," he said testily. "I just can't get them to leave us alone for five minutes. It's getting a little frustrating."

"So you're writing notes to your fiancée like you were both still in junior high?" She reached for the note again. "What does it say? *Meet me after school, but don't tell anyone?*"

Mac jammed the note into his pocket and out of her reach. "It says, *Don't tell Jessie our secret!*"

She teased him with a broad smile. "Very mature, cousin. But I'm not falling for that one. If you and Abbie had a secret, I'd have ferreted it out of her long before now. So what is it you're really trying to do? Plan your honeymoon? I think they've already got something in mind for that, too. Very thorough, those Jones brothers."

Mac wouldn't have been surprised to learn that Abbie's brothers had plotted out the first fifty years of his married life. But he wasn't interested in their long-term goals. Only those that kept him away from Abbie. "I just want a few minutes alone with Abbie away from everybody. And that includes you, too, Miss Nosy Britches."

"It's not nice to insult people when you're asking for their help, Mac."

"Jessie," he tried again, extending the note toward her. "Will you please give this note to Abbie?"

"Sure," she said with a wicked grin. "Be glad to." Then she took the note, walked across the room and handed it to Abbie.

ABBIE CLUTCHED THE PAPER in her fist and looked guilty. She could feel the tinge of guilt creeping into her cheeks. She could see the hint of it in Mac's instant frown. She could hear the inflection of it in Brad's "Woo-hoo, a love letter."

She wanted to read the note, wanted to tear it into pieces to demonstrate her disgust with men in general and her *fiancé* in particular, wanted to tell everyone she was walking out the door and no one—repeat *no one*—was ever to come looking for her again. Period. End of difficulty. Case dismissed. Over and out.

Of course, she wouldn't even be off the sofa—an action that wasn't quite as easy as it once had been—before some male or other would be offering to help her escape, drawing out maps, telling her how to pack more efficiently, thinking up places she might want to go and those she'd be better off to avoid.

Then, in a hush between her taking the note from Jessie and after her brother's gibe, Abbie realized Mac was moving toward her. He stopped right in front of her, held out his hand, and his expression said he wasn't taking no for an answer. "Will you go for a walk with me, Abbie? Right now? Just the two of us?"

There was a light stress on the "two of us," and don't-mess-with-me note of warning in his voice that was somehow directed at her brothers even though his gaze never flickered from hers. "Thank you," she said tightly. "A walk is just what I need."

Brad was on his feet, hand on her elbow, ready to help her up or knock Mac down, whichever seemed necessary. ''You mustn't get overtired, Abbie. Remember, you need to rest up for the weekend.''

''I didn't suggest we jog out to the north pasture and back,'' Mac said. ''I'll make sure she doesn't get too tired, Brad. After all, in another couple of days, taking care of Abbie will be *my* job, won't it?''

Brad helped Abbie struggle out of the cushions while he and Mac stood, locked in brother-to-lover eye contact, then he shrugged. ''Guess she's almost past needing her big brother to watch out for her, isn't she?''

''Almost,'' Mac agreed, and took Abbie's hand. ''We'll see you later.''

''You can bet on that.'' Quinn added his two cents' worth, but Abbie didn't care. Mac had finally stepped up to the plate and signaled his intention to be a player in this melodrama, a man to be reckoned with. Now all she had to do was convince him to help her, persuade him that if they faced everyone together, they could put an end to the planning, the plotting and the nonsense. All they had to do was to stand together, two people bent on managing their own affairs, united in their belief that this marriage was not going to happen.

All Abbie had to do was pretend she didn't wish in her heart of hearts that it could.

THE AIR STILL HELD the heat of the day, and the slight breeze off the water lured them toward the dock. Mac thought it was probably the worst possible choice for the discussion he had in mind. Lately he couldn't seem to even look at the lake without thinking about holding Abbie in his arms, kissing her, wanting her. His gaze dropped to the definite curve of her pregnancy beneath the oversize white shirt she wore. It was as pointless to deny that her baby was a problem between them as it was to deny the attraction that had started the first moment they'd met and had led them here, to this.

The silence walked with them like an uninvited guest, stilting the conversation before it could begin. Mac didn't know what he'd wanted so badly to say to Abbie. He didn't know what he'd thought a few minutes alone with her could accomplish. He certainly hadn't known he'd want to put his arm around her shoulders, be the buffer between her and the rest of the world, offer her the comfort of not saying a word if that was what she wanted. He hadn't realized how good it would feel just to be beside her again.

They reached the dock and Abbie walked to the side and looked at the reflection of the rising quarter moon. Nights in Texas were dark and starry, with a sky as big as a cowboy's dreams and as clear as his conscience. Mac had never before noticed how much softer and sweeter evening seemed when Abbie was in it with him. He should say something, ask her what she intended to do now, if marriage was her inevitable goal or only a means to infuse her bank account with unearned gains. But somehow, the moment was all wrong, the mood too appealing to ruin with harsh accusations and angry words. He only wanted to talk to her and hear the melodious tones of her voice in response. And yet, he couldn't speak for watching how the breeze plucked at the ribbon in her hair, for noticing the glint of gold in the moonlit strands, for knowing somehow that she needed these few minutes of peace.

"I've been rehearsing a speech for days now," she said suddenly, softly. "And now, I can't remember a word of it."

He let that sit for a moment, let the night noises have their say. "It's a wonder you had time to prepare a speech. You've been under pretty close surveillance this week."

"Me?" She almost laughed, but the sound quickly stopped, turned sober. "I've been thinking the same thing about you. It's pretty crazy that we're supposed to be getting married in a few days and no one wants us to spend two seconds alone together."

"Your brothers are trying to protect you," he offered as a completely ridiculous excuse.

"They're driving me crazy. And you've been doing your share to help them." She looked at him across the short expanse of weathered docking. "You've been avoiding me, Mac, don't deny it."

He started to, but changed his mind. "I guess I have been, in a way. I needed time to think."

"About what? The fact that in two more days we're expected to stand up in front of both our families and say we'll love and cherish each other until death do us part? Somehow, I don't believe you have to think too hard about that one."

"No."

She looked down, hesitated, then brought up her gaze and her chin in one resolute movement. "We have to tell them together,'' she said. ''It's the only way to stop this.''

''You think that will do it?''

''It will have to,'' she said firmly. Decisively. ''I don't want to marry you. You don't want to marry me. This has gone on too long already.''

She could end it here. She could tell him she was leaving. Now. Tonight. And he'd never hear from her again. ''What do you want to do, Abbie?''

''Run away,'' she said. ''Tonight. Right now. Escape without a trace. Be anywhere but here.''

Hope lifted its head, made him wonder for a second if she actually might have wearied of her charade, if she might choose to go quietly away, or if she wanted what marriage to him could give her and her baby and was simply working the conversation back around to it.

''But running away isn't the answer, either,'' she continued on a sigh, sending the hope back where it belonged. ''My parents are already on their way. They're driving, bringing God only knows what all with them. I tried to convince them not to come, that there wasn't going to be a wedding Saturday or any other day, but Quinn convinced them I was just overwhelmed by all the preparations.'' She laughed without a hint of humor. ''I am overwhelmed, Mac. And trapped.''

''I know the feeling,'' he said before he could stop himself. Her gaze narrowed, but he must have imagined the sharp flare of hurt he thought he'd seen there.

''I never set out to trap you, Mac. I know you don't believe that, but it is true.''

What would happen if he chose to believe her? What would happen if he could bring himself to trust her one more time? But why should he take her on faith? "It's simple enough to prove, Abbie."

The line of her jaw tightened. "How? By submitting my child to the indignity of a paternity test to prove to his father who he is, who he has a right to be? No, thank you. I won't sacrifice my child to your pride."

"But you'd marry me? That doesn't make any sense."

"I've just said I don't want to marry you. What is it with the men around here? You asked me to marry you for some insane reason and I said no. But somehow you persist in the belief that I didn't mean no when I said it. You—and everyone else—seems intent on believing I still intend to marry you despite numerous repetitions that it's not going to happen. I don't know what else I can possibly do or say to change your mind."

It was what had been happening all week. No one listened to Abbie. Mac had watched it, resented it, and yet, she was right, he continued to think her every word of denial was a lie, her every protest a manipulation. "You could change tactics, Abbie."

"And what would you suggest? Saying I *do* want to get married, so maybe you'll finally believe I don't? So maybe then my brothers will start undoing all the wedding plans they've put together this week?"

"Maybe."

"That would never work, Mac, and you know it.

I'm practically a prisoner as it is.'' She glanced over her shoulder, back toward the house. ''I fully expect someone will come looking for us at any second. We've been out here alone nearly ten minutes.''

''Then we'd better plan fast. What if we eloped?''

''What?''

''You heard me. We'll go along with the arrangements, we'll act happy about it, and tomorrow night, we'll elope.''

''Oh, sure, and what will that prove? That we didn't get married their way, we just got married?''

''Tomorrow night, we'll leave a note saying we decided to elope. Hopefully, that will keep them from pursuing us with any urgency. We'll make our escape, I'll drive you to the airport and see you safely off. I'll buy the ticket, get you a hotel room wherever you decide to go, and I swear no amount of torture will make me tell them where you are, until you decide to call them and tell them yourself.''

''But if I make a clean getaway, what will you do?''

He shrugged. ''Face the music. Someone has to explain. Might as well be me.''

She turned back to look out across the placid lake. ''Great idea, Mac, except for one small detail.''

''You want to go tonight instead?''

''No. The baby. What about the baby?'

Her trump card. Her any-argument topper. *What about the baby?* ''Do you want to marry me to give your baby a name, Abbie? Is that what you want?''

There was another flash of hurt in her gaze, but it was quickly overshadowed by a tightly controlled anger. "No, Mac. What I want is never to have seen you again. What I want is for none of this mess to have happened. But I did and it did and here we are. I can't go back now and pretend to myself that my baby's father is a mystery to me. I can't spend the rest of my life lying to my child about his other parent. I won't do that. I will tell the truth whether you believe it to be true or not." She inhaled quickly, deeply, seemed to regain her composure. "I need to know if you're going to make a claim on my baby later."

"Make a claim?" His voice rose with anger, too. "You've just said you wouldn't submit to a paternity test. That says to me you already know what the outcome would be." He held up a hand to stop her protest. "I haven't believed it was my baby all along, Abbie. Why would I come back after this fiasco and say it was?"

"You told your family you were the father."

"With your brothers breathing down my neck, it seemed a reasonable response. I've thought better of it since."

"I wish you'd thought better of it before you said it. But now the baby will be caught in this family tug-of-war. Do you think we can just go back to before they knew? Tell them it was all a mistake?"

His anger left as quickly as it had come. "No," he said, then again, "No."

"We have to figure this out, Mac. And the minute we do, I swear I'll get out of your life forever."

His stomach wrenched with the thought. His heart hurt at the solid-sounding forever. But his head told him to grab the opportunity she'd offered. "You go, Abbie, and I'll figure out the rest."

Even the crickets stopped chirping for the space of a heartbeat, and then another. He heard nothing other than his words, echoing like thunder, rolling in a slow, slow motion toward her and then doubling back to him. *Go, Abbie. Go, Abbie. Go, Abbie. Go...*

He felt her regret. But when she spoke there wasn't a trace of it in her voice. "All right," she said. "To-night. I'll say good-night to my brothers and I'll go to bed. At two-thirty, I'll slip out of the guest house and meet you at your truck."

"What if they catch you?"

Her expression altered, turned cruel in a humorless smile. "I'll tell them I'm sneaking out to see my *fi-ancé.*" Then as if she had no more energy to invest in what he thought of her, she lifted her shoulder in a careless shrug. "But they won't catch me, and if they do, they won't stop me."

Her determination, her confidence seemed out of place. Where had this resolve been all week? Had he finally broken her will? Or was she only manipulating him into yet another false sense of security? "What about your things?"

"My brothers will take them when they leave. They won't leave anything with you, don't worry."

"Your brothers don't worry me, Abbie. Only you."

She looked saddened by that. Her eyes held his gaze for a moment, then she turned away. "You're afraid of me," she said in a tone of soft irony. "Isn't it funny that the first time we met I ran away because

I was afraid of you, and now I have to run away because you're afraid of me."

He couldn't let that pass. "You weren't afraid of me, Abbie. You told me just the other day that you'd had a prior commitment and that's why you left without a word."

"I had accepted a job. I was going to be on my own—really on my own—for the first time in my life. It was my shot at independence, and I knew the first moment our eyes met, Mac, that I could need you forever after. You scared me all the way to the hidden corners of my soul. Running seemed the only way to save myself, so I ran, not knowing it was already too late, that I had already been caught."

He wanted to believe her. He very much wanted that. But she hadn't been caught by the need for him, but by what she believed he could give her. Wealth, status, a means to escape her authoritarian family. "It seems to me you ran because you didn't want to take any chance that your plan wouldn't work, that I'd figure out what you had in mind before you could get all your ducks in a row."

She shook her head. "What made you so distrustful, Mac? What turned your heart so hard that you'd rather believe I would scheme to rob you of some material possession than to simply want to share with you a miracle?"

"Experience."

"No, Mac. Experience teaches something of value, however painful the lesson. But all you gleaned from the fact that one woman betrayed you is that all women will do the same. You decided not to take any risk, not to trust any woman. You turned Gillian's deceit into the idea that you have no value to a woman other than as a Coleman or as a royal prince of Sorajhee. You're afraid of me because you can't believe I honestly, truly, might have loved you. You're afraid of me because you know somewhere in your stubborn, hard heart that you might have honestly, truly, loved me."

His heart clenched but somehow kept beating. She was wrong. She was playing to his sympathy, making one last attempt to change his mind, going on the offensive to maintain the upper hand. "Give it up, Abbie," he said thickly. "There's only one way you can convince me you're not just like Gillian, and that's for you to go now, tonight, and never come back."

He thought he saw her shiver, but as it wasn't cold he figured he must have imagined that, too. Certainly, he expected her to give him the cold shoulder when she realized he had won. But when she turned, there was only resolution in her expression. "I'll be at your truck at two-thirty," she said. "That should give us a three- or four-hour head start. I only wish..."

He wished, too—he just didn't know for what. "What do you wish, Abbie?"

"That I was already anyplace but here." Then she walked away from him, head up, shoulders back and, with every step, going farther out of his reach and out of his life.

Chapter Eleven

The Austin airport was eerily quiet in the early morning, as a few sleepy-looking passengers awaited the six-o'clock flight to Dallas. At other waiting areas, undoubtedly other passengers waited for other flights to arrive or leave, but the steel-and-tiled structure was mostly hushed and still. Once in a while, there was a hollow sound of hard soles on shiny tiles, of footsteps amplified by their very solitude. Abbie's disinterested gaze watched as a man ran past, his expression set and eager, indicating his lateness for a flight or in meeting a late arrival. Outside the long sweep of windows, dawn stretched lazy fingers across the horizon. Inside, the airport was bright with artificial lights and the faces of people engrossed in waiting. Some read—a newspaper, book or magazine. Some napped. Some talked to one another in low morning tones, soft and indistinguishable. Most, like Abbie, were sitting still, quietly waiting for a departure to somewhere else. She wished her plane would arrive, disembark its passengers and take her aboard. She wanted this long night to be over, these final, dreadful moments to be past. She wanted to be gone, away from Texas, away from the past few weeks, away from Mac.

He sat beside her in the waiting area for Flight 55, Southwest Airlines service from Austin to Dallas. There wasn't anything to say. Even the trip from the ranch to the airport had been completed in near silence. "Is this all you're taking?" he'd asked when she met him at the truck with her purse and a carry-on bag.

"That's it," she'd said in answer.

"Cool enough?" he'd asked on the road, offering in a gesture to adjust the air inside the truck.

"Fine, thanks," she'd replied. "Thank you" and "you're welcome" had been their only exchange after her ticket to Little Rock was purchased.

"Goodbye, Mac," she'd said once she'd checked in at the gate.

"I'll wait with you," he'd responded, as if he had to stay to make sure she got on the plane.

So, now, here they sat, side by side, not speaking at all. Two people who'd come so close to something special and ruined it so completely.

The man who'd been running came back, carrying on his shoulder a little boy who was fast asleep, talking animatedly to a woman who looked harried but happy. A family, Abbie decided. Reunited after a night of flight delays and missed connections. A father, a mother, a child. Her heart ached for what her child would miss, for the reassurance she herself might have found in sharing some of the responsibilities, all of the joys.

Mac leaned forward, elbows on his knees, hands

clasped, his hat dangling from loose fingers. The toe of his boot tapped impatiently against the carpet. His tension was high and so taut she thought if she touched him, he might snap like a rubber band, leaving her stinging from the contact. She didn't know why he was tense. She was doing what he'd wanted her to do from the start. She was going, running away like a thief in the night, as if she had something to hide, as if she had something of which to be ashamed. Mac had done that to her. Even being fired from Miss Amelia's Academy for Young Ladies hadn't made her feel this deeply humiliated. Mac had accused her of being a liar, a cheat, a master manipulator, a gold digger. He thought her guilty of the worst sort of betrayal and believed every word out of her mouth was a lie. She ought to be glad to be leaving. She ought to be anxious to get gone. But the truth was, leaving the Desert Rose had felt awful. Terrible, Wrenching.

She'd left notes for Jessie, Rose and Vi. She'd left a brief note for her brothers, telling them she needed a couple of days by herself before they came after her, before she had to explain anything. It was optimistic to think they might wait a couple of hours, but she'd done all she could and she was flat tired of trying to buck them and their better way. As long as this crazy shotgun wedding business didn't go any further, she'd take their advice about everything else. From now on, they could smother her with good intentions and she'd not say a word of protest. As long as tomorrow and Saturday passed without a wedding, she'd live the rest of her life under the suffocating shelter of their protection. It would be up to her child to exercise independence. Undoubtedly, the little one growing inside her had inherited some measure of Mac's fierce pride and the uncles would be in for a rude awakening. That thought, alone, gave Abbie's spirits a lift. Not much of one, but still a lift, to be sure.

"You're sure you want to go to Little Rock?" Mac asked all of a sudden, turning his head to look at her. "It won't give you much time to be by yourself, you know."

"Home is the best place for me to go," she said. "And with any luck at all, the boys will wait for Mom and Dad to get to the ranch later today before they all pack up and head for home. That'll give me nearly two whole days alone. It'll be enough."

He nodded, looked as if he was going to say something else, then closed his mouth and stared out the window for a moment. A plane taxied to the gate and a few minutes later, arriving passengers began to straggle out into the terminal and waiting passengers began gathering their things, listening for the announcement that it was time to board. Mac frowned, and his gaze returned to her as if he didn't have a choice. "There's one thing I'd like to know, Abbie." He hesitated, gave the hat in his hands a quarter turn, then a quarter turn back until it was positioned exactly where it had been. "When you said you could tell me and Cade apart, were you just saying that? Or did you mean it?"

She shouldn't answer. Abbie knew it was stupid to think he'd believe her now, on this one very unimportant answer, when he'd believed not another word she'd said. But wounded pride urged her to leave him with at least one little nagging question to remember her by. "I meant everything I've said to you from the beginning, Mac. And yes, I believe I could tell you from Cade no matter what the circumstances."

His expression turned skeptical but curious. "I don't see how."

"No, I don't imagine you could, because you and your twin are truly identical. But I know the difference because of the way I feel when it's you." She inhaled, wanting him to know, embarrassed by what it revealed about her feelings for him but no longer caring. She was long past the point of thinking it could make any difference. "When Cade walks into a room or talks to me or smiles at me, it's like talking to Alex or your Uncle Randy, or one of my own brothers. Nice, but nothing special. But with you, there's always a little clutch on my heart, a sense of connection, and that's how I know." She picked up her carry-on, slung her purse strap across her shoulder and stood. "Goodbye, Mac." Then, without a backward glance, she walked over, handed in her boarding pass and headed down the ramp.

At long last, and however much she might regret it, it was time for her to go home.

MAC KEPT TRYING TO BLAME his foul temper on a sleepless night. He told himself he'd done the right thing...the only thing he could do under the circumstances. By the time he reached the Desert Rose, it was well into the regular workaday routine. The morning chores were done, Stanley and Olivia were already working with their respective students, a few of the boarders were riding their horses in the outdoor arena. The sun was up and climbing, the summer heat rolling in with the promise of a sweltering afternoon. Cade was waiting at the barn, ostensibly watching the workouts, when Mac drove in.

But it wasn't difficult to ascertain he was there with an agenda and the way he turned immediately and strode over to the truck told Mac it wasn't going to be pleasant. "Where the hell have you been?" Cade asked tight-lipped. "Abbie's disappeared and her brothers are fit to be tied. We were all hoping she was with you."

"She was." Mac slammed the truck door and started for the barn. "I drove her into Austin to the airport."

"You what?"

Mac stopped, deciding to lay this on the line and be done with it. "She wanted to go and she went. There isn't going to be a wedding and that's the end of it."

"She left?"

"Yes."

Cade frowned. "What happened?"

"We talked. She said she didn't want to marry me, never wanted to marry me, and that she was leaving. So I drove her to the airport and bought her a ticket and she left." It sounded dry, emotionless, not at all the way he felt. "She won't be coming back, either."

"You okay with that?" Cade asked, his voice dipping into sympathy.

"Fine." Mac purposely responded with an uncaring syllable and a shrug. ''I'm saved from going through a wedding with a shotgun in my back. Why wouldn't I be happy?''

''You don't *look* happy.''

''Just goes to show you can't tell by looking.'' He made a move to pass his twin and go on to the barn, but Cade waylaid him.

''Go after her, Mac. She loves you. Everyone could see that, except you. Follow her. Find her. Tell her you love her and persuade her to come back here where she—and your baby—belong.''

Anger rose inside him, dark and frightening and directed completely and only at himself. ''Why would I pull a damn fool stunt like that? She's gone and I'm glad. Do you hear me? I'm glad she's gone.'' As strong as the words were, as forceful as they came out, it should have been a convincing argument. But Mac didn't come within a mile of convincing himself. ''She lied about everything, Cade. Right from the start. Even the last thing she said to me was a lie, meant to manipulate me into believing she felt something...love, maybe...when we were together.'' He snatched off his hat, ran a restless hand through his hair and shoved the hat back into place. ''She said she could tell us apart because of how she *felt* when she was with me.'' He gave a humorless laugh. ''It was a last-ditch, masterful maneuver. But not smart. Even Aunt Vi can't tell us apart when we decide to pull an identity switch. Abbie can no more tell us apart than Alex can!''

Cade pursed his lips, pushed back the brim of his hat. ''Not to burst your bubble, brother, but we couldn't fool Serena, either. We're not going to ever put this to a test, but I believe my wife when she tells me that even on the blackest night, she'd know which of us is which.''

''How?'' Mac asked, wanting to hear the reply, knowing what it would be even before his twin gave it. ''How can she tell when no one else can?''

''She says it's how she feels, the connection that isn't there with you.'' He clapped Mac on the shoulder. ''So, this time, I'm taking Abbie's side. She loves you, Mac, whether you believe her or not. If she didn't, she wouldn't have left.''

''She left because I didn't give her a choice.''

''Isn't it because you wouldn't give yourself one?''

Mac couldn't answer that. ''I have work to do,'' he said, and turned away.

''You can say that again,'' Cade nodded toward the house. ''They're all there. I'd suggest you face the music now, tell them what you've done, and get it over with.''

Mac followed the line of his brother's gaze and felt greater reluctance than he'd ever thought possible. ''I guess I'll go have a little talk with the Jones boys.''

''Not to mention Mom, Jessie and Aunt Vi. But just a word of advice, Mac. Practice looking happy before you go in there, unless you want them to know you're as miserable as you look.'' Cade turned on his heel and walked away, leaving Mac to square his shoulders and head for the next inquisition.

THERE WAS A GOOD CROWD around the long kitchen table—all of Abbie's brothers, Jessie, Rose, Vi and

Randy, Ella and Hal, Serena, Savannah and a couple of other boarders—and the mood was not at all what Mac had expected. They were laughing, several talking at once in a loop of conversation that seemed inclusive of everyone at the table…and stopped abruptly the moment he walked in.

Brad pushed back his chair and started to rise, but Tyler clapped a hand on his shoulder and they both remained seated. "Well?" Quinn voiced the question that apparently was on everyone's mind. "Where is she?"

"If she'd wanted you to know that, I guess she'd have told you in her note." Mac moved along the kitchen counter and poured himself a cup of coffee, as if that was the only answer he could, or would, provide.

"Did she tell you?" Brad asked sharply.

Mac was not going to lie about this, no matter what. "Yes," he said.

"Well, then what are you doing here?" Jaz and Jessie demanded in near unison.

"Why didn't you go after her?" Vi asked.

"We thought you'd gone after her," Serena said.

"We'll help you find her," Uncle Randy volunteered.

"Put that coffee cup down," directed Ella. "Time's a wastin'."

"She's got to be back here in time for the wedding," Quinn stated forcefully.

Mac stopped the runaway comments with a look. "She isn't coming back. I'm not going after her. We aren't getting married."

For a second, there was silence. Then a cacophony of disbelief, which Mac ended with a sharp, ''Stop it! When I asked Abbie to marry me, she said no. She meant no. No. Could that be any clearer?''

''You don't know her like we do,'' Tyler said.

''She hasn't known what she wanted since she was a kid,'' Brad said.

''She's pregnant,'' Quinn said. ''You have to marry her.''

Mac looked from the face of one brother to another. ''Have the four of you ever listened to a word Abbie says? Have you ever given her the benefit of the doubt? Just once?''

''We're her family.'' Brad shrugged off Ty's restraining hand and pushed to his feet. ''We want her to have what she deserves.''

Anger returned, flooding Mac with confidence this time. ''She *deserves* to be heard. She *deserves* to make her own decisions, regardless of whether or not the four of you agree with them. And when she says something, she *deserves* to be *believed.*''

The sheer force of the words drove into the air, but it was Mac who nearly fell backward from the impact. *She deserves to be believed. She deserves to be believed.* She *deserves to be believed.* Abbie had said the baby was his. She had said she didn't set out to trap him. She had said she didn't want a loveless marriage. She had said she could tell who he was simply by the way she felt when she was with him. And until this moment when the words left his mouth, he hadn't known he believed her.

''So what do you wish to do, Makin?'' Rose asked

softly, comfortingly, her mother love reaching across the kitchen toward him, as it had been reaching toward him all those years from the cells of her prison. ''Should we cancel the wedding?''

It was, he realized, the last thing he wanted. He loved Abbie. He believed her. He wanted to be her husband and a father to their child. She had said it best when she told him he hadn't learned anything from his experience with Gillian if it meant he couldn't tell the difference between a deceitful heart and real love. He'd lived in such fear of treachery that he'd fulfilled the expectation and betrayed his own heart, and hers. ''I'm going after her,'' he said, sure suddenly it was the right thing to do. ''I'll bring her back if I can.''

''We'll go with you,'' Quinn offered. ''We'll make her see she needs to come back, for the baby's sake.''

''Just tell us where she is,'' Brad said. ''We'll be sure she's back in time for the wedding tomorrow.''

It felt good to be able to say, ''No. I love her. She's having my baby. It's my responsibility to find her and ask her what she wants.''

''You have a lot to learn about our sister,'' Tyler suggested, shaking his head. ''You have to tell Abbie what she needs to do. She's not much of a decision maker.''

''She will be from now on,'' Mac said, eyeing each of her brothers in turn. ''I do have a lot to learn about Abbie, that's true. But I can tell you this much, she's an intelligent, rational and wonderful woman who deserves to make her own choices, and I'm going to do everything in my power to make sure she does.''

Then grabbing his hat, he made eye contact with Jessica and asked her without words to follow him. He needed Abbie's address in Little Rock, because he'd go door-to-door throughout the city before he'd give away her hiding place by asking her brothers for directions.

ABBIE COULDN'T REMEMBER ever being alone in her parents' house before, and she wandered from room to room, aimlessly recalling holidays and other times in this sprawling but graceful place she'd always known as home. She could remember admiring the model airplanes in Quinn's room, the meticulously painted soldiers and warships in Brad's. She'd browsed the books and comics stacked in neat piles around Jaz's bed and she'd played endless hours with Tyler's collection of cars, trucks and things that go. Her room was still much as it had been before she'd left for college—pink, frilly, fussy with a few traces of a little girl trying hard to grow up. It was, she thought, partly her fault that she'd never taken a solid stand against her brothers' meddling. Certainly her parents had offered at least some support for her claiming of independence, but she was the baby of the family, the only girl after four rowdy, death-defying, arrogant and endearing boys. They'd watched out for her before she learned to walk. They'd adored her from the start and wanted nothing but to protect her.

She should have started early if she'd truly wanted to be independent of them. She should have learned how to wrap them around her little finger instead of going along with all their plans since she was old enough to talk. She should have done so many things she hadn't done. With a sigh, Abbie sank onto the powder-puff pink bedspread in her room and looked at the fashion statements of her own Barbie collection. Placing her hands on her stomach, she pushed in lightly and felt the baby kick out in response. No way would this little one let someone else direct her life. She—Abbie was beginning to think of the baby as a girl—wouldn't let her uncles dictate to her. No sir. She would have her father's fire, as well as his dark eyes and regal carriage. No one would dare tell Mac Coleman's daughter what she ought to do. Abbie thought it might be a tough ride from time to time, but when this newest Sorajheean princess was grown, she'd be strong and sure and fiercely wonderful. And for that alone, Abbie couldn't regret what had already come to pass.

She'd made it all the way to Little Rock alone. She'd taken a cab to the house, let herself in with the key her family insisted she always carry with her, made herself eat a meal, even if it had tasted mainly like cardboard. Then she'd slept several hours and awakened to roam the silent house, waiting for the inevitable stampede of brothers. Probably parents, too. The Joneses would definitely put in their share of traveling miles this week. But in the future, Abbie figured they'd all stay pretty close to this house, the home they all kept coming back to. Over the years, her brothers had moved out, gone on to pursue their own interests, but they gathered here routinely, and Abbie wondered if taking care of her had somehow provided them an acceptable excuse to postpone starting their own homes, their own families. Were her brothers perhaps, in their own way, as afraid of making that commitment to love as she had been with Mac?

It was an interesting thought and Abbie might have considered it further if the doorbell hadn't rung just then. With a sigh, she pushed up from the edge of the bed, figuring they'd rung the doorbell only to give her fair warning before they unlocked the door and burst in around her in a plethora of affectionate chastisements and reprimands. But when she reached the entry hall, there was only a single silhouette on the other side of the sheer curtains that covered the half glass of the front door. Her heart gave a funny little clutch, told her even before she turned the knob and pulled open the door that Mac was standing on the porch. His hat was in his hands, as it had been when she'd left him in the airport. His hair was disheveled, his clothes the same ones he'd worn this morning, and his eyes showed the weight of whatever he'd come here to say. He looked tired, worried, scared and arrogantly determined not to show it.

"Mac," she whispered, happy just to see him, despite having every reason not to be. "What are you doing here?"

"I love you," he said in a voice that betrayed his tight attempt at controlling his emotion. "Will you marry me?"

Abbie blinked. "What?"

"I love you," he repeated. "Will you marry me?"

She frowned, looked past him. "Where are they?" she asked, sure her brothers were there somewhere, certain they'd convinced him this was what he had to do. "My brothers put you up to this, didn't they?"

"No." Mac gave a barely noticeable shake of his head. "They don't know you're here. I didn't tell them where you'd gone. I told you I wouldn't."

"Yes, I know, but they can be very persuasive."

"Abbie, I like your brothers, but they couldn't persuade me to take off my hat if it wasn't what I wanted to do."

She wouldn't allow herself to project out the meaning of that statement, denied herself the seed of hope stirring in her heart. "But you asked me to marry you."

"And you haven't answered."

"I said no the last time."

"I remember. If you say no this time, I'll respect that, but I reserve the right to try and change your mind."

This was strange. Wonderful, maybe, too. Or not. Abbie didn't know what to think. "Do you want to come inside? It's hot out there."

"It's hotter in Texas," he said, and she laughed, a soft, nervous, happy sound.

"Yes," she agreed, "it is, but it's hot enough here, so come in. Please." He hesitated and she encouraged him with a wry smile. "I promise there's no one here waiting to jump out and accuse you of ruining my already tattered reputation."

"I'm sorry, Abbie. I've made a real mess of things."

"You?" She shook her head. "I think I'm the one at fault here."

He started to contradict her, but stopped. "I don't

want to tell you what to think, or how you feel. I came here because I realized how unfair I'd been to you and I wanted to tell you I wish I could go back to that first day at the airport and start all over with you. I had no reason to believe you were lying. I was just so afraid that you didn't, couldn't, love me that I set out to put up high jumps you couldn't possibly clear, so I'd be safe from disappointment. But that was wrong, Abbie. Wrong of me and wrong for me. I love you. I've been in love with you since the first moment I saw you. The fact that we're going to have a child...well, I'd be lying if I said I wasn't a little scared at the idea of becoming a father. But that doesn't mean I won't give it my best shot.'' He stopped, swallowed a knot of emotion in his throat, then continued. ''I love you, Abbie. Will you marry me?''

She forgave him in the space of a heartbeat but wasn't quite ready to tell him so. ''You know, this is my second proposal—third, if you count Andy Perkins in first grade—and I'm wondering if they all have to be supervised.'' She nodded at the cab, still sitting at the curb, the driver peering at them through the open window. ''I'm beginning to think a marriage proposal is a spectator sport.''

Mac glanced around, brought his gaze back to her. ''I guess Andy proposed in front of the whole class?''

''During the Christmas program, in fact, in front of practically the whole school and all the parents.''

Mac frowned. ''What did your brothers do to him?''

''I don't know. Probably scared the dickens out of him. Andy never talked to me again after that, although I think I remember some rather soulful stares."

"Maybe I should come inside and start this proposal business over again."

She stepped back. "Good idea."

But the moment he stepped over the threshold, Abbie didn't give him a chance to propose. She didn't even bother to shut the door. She simply went into his arms and lifted her face for his kiss. What difference did it make if the taxi driver was watching? She wouldn't care if the whole world saw. She loved Mac and she was going to marry Mac. They were having a baby. And however this miracle had come about, she knew the truth had finally won out.

A long time later, after the door was closed and locked, after their lips were swollen and warm with kisses, after their bodies had spoken of a future their voices had yet to claim, Mac knelt before her and said again, "I love you, Abbie. Will you marry me?"

"Yes," she said. "Yes."

And her proud Arabian prince bowed his head against her hand and breathed a sigh of relief. "Thank you. I know I don't deserve this second chance, Abbie, but I will be grateful every day for the rest of my life that you gave it to me."

"You may regret it when my brothers drive us crazy with their interference. They'll be doting uncles, I'm afraid."

"Even if they try to move in with us—which we will not allow—I promise you I will never regret this choice. You are my sun, my moon, my stars, and I'll do everything in my power to make you happy."

"You did that, Mac, the moment I opened the front door."

He grinned. "I hate to even mention this, but we should probably call in and let everyone know we're okay. Otherwise…"

"…they'll all be here by morning." She ran her fingertips across his strong, handsome jaw. "I suppose we could call and tell them we're on our way to Las Vegas and one of the wedding chapels there."

"We could. But if you wouldn't mind, I'd like to marry you at the little church in Bridle, in front of your family and mine. If that's what you'd like, too."

Of course. The wedding should be there, in the beautiful hill country of Texas, where Mac had become the proud Texas sheikh he was at this moment, where their own child would grow up and become whoever she was meant to be. "I'd like that, Mac. I'd like that very much. And since our families have already gone to all the trouble of planning a wedding, we may as well show up for it, don't you think?"

"Wouldn't you rather plan a wedding yourself?"

She laughed, not caring a whit if someone else had decided what, when and where their wedding would be. "I think it's a little late for me to worry about the small stuff. In a couple of months, I'll have my hands full with your son or daughter. Believe me, the details of the wedding aren't what I want to spend my energy on. I'd much rather spend my time honeymooning with my husband in the guest house by the lake."

His smile made her fall in love with him all over again. "A perfect plan, Miss Jones…soon to be Mrs. Coleman-El Jeved, or if you prefer, I'll just call you Princess Abigail."

"Save the princess title for our daughter. I'll just stay plain Abbie."

"Beautiful Abbie," he corrected, teasing her lips with a soft kiss. "My beautiful, independent wife."

"First wife. And only wife. I'm afraid I must insist on your late father's tradition of having no harem."

He grinned. "If you think I'm going to have time for any other women, you have greatly exaggerated my potential as a husband."

"It's true, I'm planning to keep you very busy." She paused, feeling humbled and yet empowered by his love. "Have you noticed how full of plans I am, all of a sudden?"

He kissed her nose and stood. Extending a hand, he pulled her to her feet. "But if you don't focus your organizational skills on getting us back to Texas by tomorrow morning, we're going to miss our own wedding."

"Consider it done, my love. Consider it done."

THE CHURCH WAS A GARDEN of fresh flowers and shimmering candles. Jessica, Serena and Hannah were in dresses of a lavender hue and carried bouquets of yellow and pink roses as they walked down the aisle. Mac, with Cade, Alex and Nick Grayson beside him, stood at the front of the long aisle, dressed in black jeans, black boots, white shirt, tuxedo coat and tie. The chimes of the organ sounded out the beginning of "The Wedding March" and the doors opened to reveal Abbie, dressed in flowing, high-waisted ivory satin, on her father's arm.

Mac hadn't expected the flood of emotion that filled him at that moment, but he knew it was right and good. From this day forward, he would place his trust and faith in Abbie and they would build a home and a life together. Their children would be born, knowing that despite a rocky beginning, they had been conceived in a love that was meant to be.

As Abbie reached his side and they turned together to face each other, Mac reached for her hand.

And miracle of miracles, she gave it to him.

THE RECEPTION LASTED even after the bride and groom had retreated to the guest house, where they planned to stay until—and this was given as a direct warning—they decided to come out. Abbie had said goodbye to her brothers, promised she'd report to them the moment her labor began, spent a little quality time with her parents and kept her hand in Mac's the entire time.

Randy had never seen his nephew so happy and marveled at the turn of events that had shifted all their lives in the past year. It had been quite a year for the Colemans. Rose was back with them, reunited with him and Vi and with her three sons. They'd had three weddings in six months. Within the next few months, there'd be the birth of Mac and Abbie's baby, then Vi's and Jessica's mutual birthday. Savannah was doing a great job getting the details of that surprise together. Then sometime early next year, Hannah and Alex would have their twins and there would be three babies to carry the Coleman-El Jeved legacy into another generation. Who knew what other events might come to pass in this ongoing cycle of living? Randy was enjoying this wild rush into the future, even as he wished he might slow it down a bit and have a little more time to enjoy events, like his nephew's wedding. He looked around, noted the crowd was thinning, the food nearly gone, and he decided he'd grab two glasses and a bottle of champagne and see if he couldn't persuade Vi to join him in a private toast.

"Hey, Dad." Jessie walked up behind him. "Jared Grayson is looking for you. Says he needs to warn you about something. Maybe he's decided to disown his worthless son and wants to give you a heads-up."

"Jessie," Randy said, weary with his daughter's determination to dislike Nick, who was—in Randy's view—a remarkable and extremely likable young man. "If you keep saying stuff like that about Nick, I'm going to have to start thinking it's because you have a secret passion for him."

She choked on a broccoli bite, glared at him, her mismatched eyes equally perturbed by his comment. "As if that would happen if he was the only man left on this planet," she snapped, and marched indignantly off to tell someone else how much she disliked Nick Grayson.

Randy smiled at the thought that it would take a man like Nick to handle Jessie. But then, as he saw Jared approaching, the smile changed to that of pleasure in a long-standing friendship. "I'm so glad you and Nick made it for the wedding," he said. "Means a lot to me and Vi. Rose, too, but she probably told you that herself."

"She did," Jared agreed. "Beautiful wedding. And a baby coming soon. The Desert Rose enterprise is growing by leaps and bounds. Which is what I wanted to tell you. Just before Nick and I left Dallas, I received a call from a reporter at the *Dallas Morning News.* Seems there's a rumor afloat that Balahar royalty—I'm taking that to mean King Zak and his son, Crown Prince Sharif—are making a secret trip to Texas to look at the Desert Rose stock. I figured we'd have some flare-up of nosy reporters the first few times King Zak came to visit Serena, but from the questions the reporter was asking, seems to me you need to be on the lookout for more reporters at the Desert Rose."

Randy sighed. They'd barely recovered from the last bunch of nosy newsmen and now it'd start all over again. The only reason no one had been here to cover the wedding today was because the whole thing had happened too fast for the papers to get wind of it. "Well, I wish they'd leave the boys alone, but I guess the idea of a story about three princes raised to be Texas sheikhs is just too great."

Jared laughed. "Maybe you'll get lucky and some other unfortunate royalty will do something to snag the media's attention. But come what may, Randy, we'll weather the storm and Coleman-Grayson will head on into the future, which you know as well as I do, looks very bright."

Randy nodded. "It does indeed, Jared. It does, indeed."

ABBIE TRAILED KISSES from her husband's lips to his bare chest, then nestled against him amidst the tangled sheets. Her naked body cupped his with utter contentment and a happiness still too new to feel entirely real. But Mac was real. As were the soft, fluttery kicks of their baby in her womb. The last time she and Mac had shared this bed in the guest house, none of this had seemed possible. What a difference a day made.

"A penny for your thoughts," he said, his voice a throaty vibration under her cheek.

"I was just thinking how happy I am to be here with you. We may have done this somewhat backward, but the important thing is that we ended up at the right place."

He traced her lips with a gentle fingertip. "Not ended, Abbie. Begun. We're beginning at exactly the right place. For you, for me and for our baby."

"I guess it's true, then," she said, smiling as he gathered her closer into the solid shelter of his arms. "Real love stories never have endings, only a lifetime of happily ever afters."

"A lifetime," he agreed, kissing the top of her head. "And then some."

* * * * *

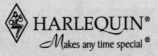

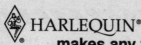

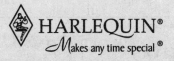

Harlequin invites you to walk down the aisle . . .

To honor our year long celebration of weddings we are offering an exciting opportunity for you t own the Harlequin Bride Doll. Handcrafted i fine bisque porcelain, the wedding doll is dresse for her wedding day in a cream satin gow accented by lace trim. She carries an exquisit traditional bridal bouquet and wears a cathedral length dotted Swiss veil. Embroidered flowe cascade down her lace overskirt to the scallope hemline; underneath all is a multi-layered crinoline

Join us in our celebration of weddings by sending away for you own Harlequin Bride Doll. This doll regularly retails for $74.95 U.S./approx. $108.6 CDN. One doll per household. Requests must be received no later than Decembe 31, 2001. Offer good while quantities of gifts last. Please allow 6-8 weeks for deliver Offer good in the U.S. and Canada only. Become part of this exciting offer!

Simply complete the order form and mail to:
"A Walk Down the Aisle"

IN U.S.A	IN CANADA
P.O. Box 9057	P.O. Box 622
3010 Walden Ave.	Fort Erie, Ontario
Buffalo, NY 14269-9057	L2A 5X3

Enclosed are eight (8) proofs of purchase found in the last pages o every specially marked Harlequin series book and $3.75 check o money order (for postage and handling). Please send my Harlequi Bride Doll to:

Name (PLEASE PRINT)

Address Apt. #

City State/Prov. Zip/Postal Code

Account # (if applicable) **097 KIK DAEW**

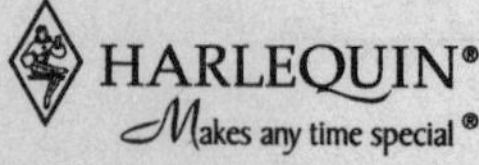

Visit us at www.eHarlequin.com

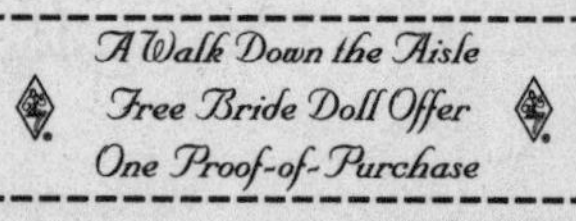

PHWDAPOPR2